Someone piped up, "You aim to arrest someone in this very room?" Longarm nodded in answer. His eyes locked with his quarry. Once again he had that old and all too familiar feeling of weary disgust and cold fear as he somehow sensed what was coming. He tried to keep it clean.

He said to the killer in disguise, "I suspect I know what you're thinking and you'd better think again. This is real life and stage acting ain't about to cut the mustard."

He saw the hesitation in the other man's eyes as the crowded room fell silent as a tomb. The true secret of the gunfighter was in going with your instincts when they told you the other fool really meant it. So Longarm was ready when the ashen-faced killer went for his gun. Longarm drew and fired just once—in hopes of taking at least one of the bastards alive . . .

◆→ TABOR EVANS ◆→

LONGARM

AND THE DEAD RINGERS

J

JOVE BOOKS, NEW YORK

LONGARM AND THE DEAD RINGERS

A Jove Book / published by arrangement with the author

PRINTING HISTORY
Jove edition / December 1993

ISBN: 0-515-11255-0

A JOVE BOOK®
Jove Books are published by The Berkley Publishing Group,
200 Madison Avenue, New York, New York 10016.
JOVE and the "J" design are trademarks
belonging to Jove Publications, Inc.

PRINTED IN THE UNITED STATES OF AMERICA

10 9 8 7 6 5 4 3 2 1

Chapter 1

U.S. Deputy Marshal Custis Long had been reporting for work on time so often that his friends and foes around the Denver Federal Building were starting to wonder about him.

Longarm, as he was better known, was a tad concerned about other changes in his usual habits since pretty Edwina Rose had somehow wound up sharing his hired quarters on the unfashionable side of Cherry Creek. For as some wise French philosopher had doubtless inscribed in stone, every man hopes the gal of his dreams will stay just the way she is the first time he grabs hold of her, while every woman hopes to change her man just a teeny little bit, assuring both of them considerable disappointment.

So he'd told Edwina Rose more than once how much he hated starch in his collars, and warned her the tobacco-brown tweed of his store-bought suit had never been meant to be dry-cleaned all that often. But she seemed to be one of those gals who could turn her ears off after she'd laughed like hell at all a man's jokes the first couple of times. And it was funny how he'd never noticed before that nasal whine in the pretty little thing's contralto as she nagged him, at the damnedest times, to do the damnedest things.

They were going at it dog-style by the dawn's early light, lest either be late for work after all the washing up and fussing Edwina Rose insisted on afterwards, bless her tidy nature, when she archly asked him, as he was clinging to her bare hips and rapidly ramming between her bare buttocks, whether he meant to demand that raise, as he'd "promee-womeed," from that stingy old Marshal Vail as soon as he got to his office.

Longarm had promised no such thing. He'd tried to tell her Marshal William Vail of the Denver District Court had no say in either wages or per diems paid out by the Justice Department under the sound money policies of President Rutherford B. Hayes, bless his thrifty nature.

But her unreasonable demands at such a moment of natural male weakness reminded him of other demands by a far less desirable female. So he shoved it in as deep as they could manage and replied, as well as a man could through clenched teeth, "Speaking of my perilous finances reminds me. My landlady's been asking about us. I mean, she's taken to cornering me in the vestibule after work with stuck-up comments about the respectable sort of boarding house she likes to think she runs—or at least about an adjustment in my rent if I mean to make a habit of sharing my single quarters with overnight guests."

Edwina Rose bit her lower lip and shuddered in orgasm, while he lost the thread of their conversation for a spell as well. But after they got their breathing back, lying sideways across the rumpled bedding as his erection subsided inside her, Edwina Rose said, "I could lend you some money-wunny till you get that raise, honey-bunny."

Longarm felt his sated shaft shrivel all the way out of her as he firmly replied, "Not hardly. Thanks all the same. I'll ask Billy Vail to put me in for more money the next time I get him to feeling guilty. I can look mighty morose when he

2

sends me out in the field with snow in the air and so close to harvest time."

She stiffened her naked spine against his bare belly as she sort of hissed, "Don't you dare go off chasing outlaws on me with the fall social season coming on, Custis Long! I told you we had invitations to the Harvest Moon Cotillion, and surely you can get us invited to that G.A.R. Ball out at Camp Weld, seeing you rode in the war and all."

He sighed and replied, "I never joined no veterans' groups once I got out of the tedious mess. It sure beats me how many old boys who'd pined for the day they could turn their backs on army life forever get all gussied up in Union blue or Confederate gray to celebrate the times they'd said they hated so much. I forget what I did with my old uniform. Don't even recall whether it was blue or gray. Only remember it was a lot more ragged and I was a lot older and wiser than I was when first they issued it to me with a rifled musket and socket bayonet."

She wasn't listening, of course. She was already up and washing all over at the corner washstand, the way working gals tended to do by the logical light of an early weekday morn.

Longarm propped himself up on one elbow to reach for the shirt he'd hung over the back of a bedside chair. Edwina Rose said, without turning from the mirror, "You don't intend to wear the same shirt two days in a row, do you, darling?"

He soberly replied, "Perish the thought. I was reaching for my tobacco and a light. But since you brought it up, Edwina Rose, they told me over to my usual Chinee laundry that you never left my stuff there the way you said you would the other day."

She began to brush her long dark hair, her shapely rear view teasing him, as she sniffed and said, "I've found a new

3

laundry. I didn't like the way that little Oriental harlot bats her squinty eyes at you, dear."

He almost let go of the three-for-a-nickel cheroot between his teeth, and even forgot to light it, as he laughed incredulously and asked, "Might we be talking about bitty Ming Ling, fourteen years of age soaking wet and mighty good at ironing hickory shirts without starch?"

Edwina Rose sniffed some more and said, "They seem to mature early in the parts of the world where such people really belong. Suffice it to say, the laundry closer to my own boardinghouse does a better job. I told them you *do* need starch, in just the collars and cuffs at least. How do you expect them to promote you to the position you deserve if you wander in at all hours looking like a cowboy, dear?"

He lit his cheroot, grumbling about nobody ever riding drag in any infernal starched shirt when he was herding cows with Captain Midnight just after the war.

She said they'd talk about it later, when he picked her up after work at her own boardinghouse. When she suggested he show up with some flowers that evening, lest the other young ladies there think he was taking her for granted, Longarm let smoke trickle thoughtfully out both nostrils and replied, "I ain't sure I'll be able to make it with or without the posies, honey. My ornery old boss said something about sending me off to Leadville, or was it Fort Collins? Anyways, it was something about interference with the U.S. mails, and we like to give the Post Office inspectors a hand from time to time."

She whirled from the mirror, an interesting sight with her proud breasts still bare, and firmly stated, "I'm going to that Harvest Moon Cotillion this weekend, Custis Long, with or without you as my escort! It's not as if I never told you we had tickets well in advance, you know!"

He nodded gravely. "I mean to point that out to Marshal

Billy Vail if he picks me instead of a less serious-minded deputy. But you just said yourself you wanted me to ask for a raise and . . ."

He let it go as she began to haul duds on over her head, not really interested in anything he might have to say that didn't agree with her.

So he got dressed in the time it took such a handsome gal to pin a proper hat atop her properly pinned-up hair, and as luck or common courtesy would have it, none of the other roomers were out prowling the halls and stairwell as he whisked Edwina Rose downstairs and all the way to the Larimer Street Bridge across Cherry Creek, where they kissed and parted company discreetly lest people talk at either of their downtown office buildings.

Longarm paused for tamales wrapped in newsprint as well as corn husks, stopped for a morning pick-me-up at the Parthenon Saloon near the Federal Building, and still made it up to the damned office a few minutes early.

Old Henry, the young squirt who played the typewriter out front, was a kiss-ass who was often waiting at the door like a lost pup when Marshal Vail showed up in the cold gray dawn with the keys. So Longarm wasn't surprised to see him sitting at his desk. But Henry stared up surprised and demanded, "What happened? Her husband got back from that buying trip to Omaha earlier than expected?"

Longarm hadn't thought that was so funny the first time Henry had come up with it. But he smiled anyway and confided, "She's out to *get* herself a husband *poco tiempo,* and I'd as soon it was some other Cotillion dancer. So no shit, Henry, don't we have, say, a federal want on some suspect rumored to be dealing faro in Frisco, or mayhaps casino in K.C.?"

Henry managed to sound almost as prim as Edwina Rose as he replied, "It's not my fault you've been pulling courtroom duty down the hall for so long. None of the other deputies have taken to showing up in fresh-pressed suits and starched collars of late. I did place an envelope I never opened, from some sheriff's department in Montana, I think, with the other morning mail inside."

Longarm was already moving as Henry added, "It was stamped with a county seal and marked personal, so I just put it on top and . . ."

Longarm knocked once to be polite and barged on in without waiting for an invitation. So the somewhat older and far shorter and stouter Billy Vail glanced up from behind his cluttered desk at one end of his oak-paneled inner office to growl, "I was just thinking about you. Got a mighty odd message from an old-timer you might remember."

Longarm said flatly, "I'll go. Just tell me where and who you want me to bring in, Boss."

Vail scowled impatiently from beneath his bushy brows. "How many times do I have to tell you not to interrupt your elders?"

So Longarm sat down uninvited, and leaned back in the one leather guest chair as Vail continued. "Old Walt Wallward was your elder too when first you signed on with us as a junior deputy six or eight years back. But you remember him, don't you?"

Longarm lit a fresh cheroot as he pondered how he ought to answer. He'd gotten along tolerably with the cuss. It had been Vail's idea to hand Wallward the shovel after he'd reported in drunk just one time too often.

Shaking out the match, Longarm settled for simply saying he did recall the ex-deputy in question. So Vail said, "Watch what you do with them ashes, you sloppy young jasper. I fired Walt Wallward and I make no apologies for calling the man a useless drunk at the time. He *was* a useless drunk at the time and I had to get rid of him before he got shot or worse

6

yet, shot somebody innocent. But I was happy to learn way later how the love of a good woman had turned the doomed soul around and got him to sign the pledge before somebody killed him, or vice versa."

Longarm let out a smoky sigh of relief. "Sometimes a gal can really have a good influence on a man. I'm glad old Walt got over being such a disgusting drunk. He seemed a good old boy when he was halfway sober."

Vail nodded. "Good tracker too. One of the best deputies I ever had when he was off the sauce. I reckon that's how come they elected him sheriff up Montana way when they incorporated a couple of the more settled counties in the territory after the big Sioux scare of '76."

Vail waved the four-page letter in one hand as he continued. "He says he recalls you fondly as a promising junior deputy who rode out after the owlhoot Plowright boys with him that time. Do you recall that case, old son?"

Longarm removed his damned hat to flick the damned ashes in it because the damned rug had just been cleaned. "Well, sure I remember, Billy. It was one of my first hot pursuits, and ain't it odd how a man remembers his first screwings and his early gunfights clear as hell? I disremember the name of a lady I met up near Ward last summer, but I can still see the print dress little Sally May peeled out of in that West-by-God-Virginia hayloft, and I remember how young Bob Plowright smiled at me sort of wistful and said, 'Aw, now look what you've done to my new shirt!' just before he threw up his lungs at my feet that day in Julesberg."

Billy Vail nodded soberly. "In my case her name was Jo Ann, and a Mex I had to gun early on called my mama mean things in his own lingo. Now that you mention it, his shirt was tomato red and there was this boil on his neck. But getting back to Sheriff Walter Wallward. You were there to witness his shooting the oldest Plowright boy a good five times fatally as he was tear-assing up the street aboard a doubtless mighty spooked bronc."

Longarm nodded. "It was a bay gelding with four white stockings. Belonged to one of the innocents drinking in the saloon a few doors down from the house of ill repute the Plowright boys had been staying in. Walt Wallward, being sober as well as senior to me at the time, posted me and . . . right, Deputies McEwen and Pope in the side alley to cover that way out. Bob and Jim Plowright came boiling out that way guns blazing about two seconds after old Walt banged authoritatively on the front door."

Dropping more ash in his hat, Longarm continued thoughtfully. "Jim Plowright died instantly. Bob took a few moments to cough up his lungs for us, like I said. Their big brother, Tall Tom Plowright, dove headfirst through a bay window next to the front door Walt was banging on to roll through the picket fence, dash along the walk as far as the first tethered pony he came to, and leave town in a hail of bullets. Me, McEwen, and Pope got off a few rounds ourselves as he vanished down the street in the dust. Walt Wallward had started sooner and emptied his five chambers by the time the rest of us made it out front. So it's likely he was the one who killed the acrobatic son of a bitch."

Taking another drag on his cheroot he went on. "A farmer down the road a piece found the last of the Plowrights dead in his dooryard later, and brought him back into town for the bounty, the lucky cuss. I recall Walt Wallward taking it sort of hard, with whiskey, even though some of the others tried to tell him you frowned on your deputies claiming bounty money for just doing their jobs."

Longarm quickly added, "I can say he got drunk that night now that he's taken the pledge and don't work for you no more in any case. I suspect he was more upset about not getting full credit than he was about that farmer claiming the price on Tall Tom's head seeing the posters read dead or alive."

Billy Vail waved the pages of the letter impatiently. "He told me all that at the time. Once I got him sobered up. Claimed the rounds dug out of Tall Tom's kidney, liver, and lights, four in all, came from the wheel of his very own Schofield. And who was I to argue though they dug three rounds of Army .45 and a .44 slug out of the cadaver? Is the point to be made that Tall Tom Plowright was brought in dead and lies buried in or about the town of Julesberg, Colorado, even as we speak?"

Longarm nodded. "To be specific, betwixt his two brothers in the southeast quadrant of that potter's field out past the stockyards. I was there. It seemed only decent since none of their kith or kin showed up for their burials. The three of 'em hailed from far-off Ohio before they went wrong, didn't they?"

Vail said, "You do have a memory for first loves. I'd have to look that up. You'd know Tall Tom Plowright if you saw him today, though, wouldn't you?"

Longarm grimaced. "I wouldn't bet on that. He's been in the ground unembalmed for eight or ten years, Billy."

Vail said, "Seven, according to Walt Wallward, who's been looking things up a lot of late. My question was meant to deal with Tall Tom Plowright if he was to, say, walk through that door there right this minute."

"He won't," said Longarm flatly. "I paid my last respects to him and his brothers as the three of 'em lay under a sunny sky in open caskets. I had already ridden through one war so, young as I may have been at the time, I knew a dead man from a sleeping beauty and Tall Tom Plowright was sincerely dead, after an autopsy to determine where each and every bullet had wound up in him. You know that waxy look they get, along with them liverish blotches where blood pools along the bottom side of a corpse?"

Vail nodded. "Lividity. Useful in showing whether a dead body's been moved after it's lain dead a spell."

Longarm said, "That farmer brought Tall Tom in facedown, across a packsaddle. Said he'd been laying facedown in the dooryard earlier. Anyway, he sure looked deader than average, staring up at us with his open mouth abuzz with flies and his features all bruised-looking. I'll never forget what he looked like. But I'd sure be surprised if I ever *saw* him again."

Vail hesitated, then said tersely, "Sheriff Walter Wallward writes it gave *him* quite a turn too. He says Tall Tom Plowright seems to be up and about up Montana way, menacing the hell out of him and everybody old enough to recall the wicked ways of the Plowright gang."

Longarm took another drag on his smoke, sighed, and said, "I'm sure sorry to hear poor old Walt's taken to demon rum some more. So far I never have, but they do say gents see all sorts of odd sights after a few years of serious drinking."

Vail nodded. "That's the first thing I considered. So I wired my opposite number at the Helena District Court. They wired me Sheriff Walter Wallright enjoys a rep for sobriety as well as slick tracking. His county seat's just down the Missouri headwaters from the territorial capital and so jurisdictions tend to overlap. They report they've heard of other sightings, and asked me to send them any outstanding federal warrants we might have on Tall Tom Plowright."

Reaching for his own cigar, as if in self-defense, Vail added, "Needless to say, we don't have any. We generally close the books on a case when all the possible culprits are dead, or seem to be dead. You're sure that was Tall Tom Plowright you saw all the way to his grave up Julesberg way that time, old son?"

Longarm shrugged. "Nope. I said I gunned Bob Plowright personally, and saw old boys reputed to be James and Thomas Plowright getting shot at by others. I know for a fact it was Bob Plowright I had to shoot because I went through his pockets after he was dead. I fail to see what those other gents could have been up to so close to him if they hadn't been the brothers we all took them for."

Vail's cigar was shorter and fatter than Longarm's cheroot too. As he lit it, Longarm asked, "You say this live cuss claiming to be the late Tall Tom has been *menacing* folk up Montana way, Billy? How might an owlhoot rider killed seven years back go about menacing a sane and sober citizen today?"

Billy Vail let fly a smoke signal suitable for a Cheyenne rising and snorted, "By not being dead, of course! How would you like to be a sobered-up drunk, running for re-election this November, with a famous outlaw you were famous for gunning offering to buy you a drink at the saloon across the damned street from your damned sheriff's office?"

Longarm smiled thinly at the picture. "There you go. I got it figured from here in this chair without a damned ashtray. You just now said it was an election year, and we all know what some sneaky rascals will do to get elected, or keep others from licking them fair and square at the ballot boxes."

Vail scowled through the blue haze that now filled the room as he demanded, "You're suggesting even a crook-ed politician would revive a dead outlaw just to swing an election?"

Longarm shook his head morosely. "Crooked politician is a redundancy, like saying sweet honey or smelly shit, and nobody this side of the Good Book can revive the dead no matter what Mrs. Shelley wrote in her book about Doc Frankenstein. But haven't we caught crooks out to spook

Indians with made-up haunts, or swindle rightful heirs by claiming to be long-lost kin?"

Vail blew more smoke his way. "Walt Wallward says the man wandering about up yonder looks just like Tall Tom, talks just like Tall Tom, and claims to *be* Tall Tom. He went to a newspaper office the first day he rode in to tell them their sheriff's tale of having shot it out with the Plowright boys that time in Julesberg was a pure plate of tripe."

Longarm nodded and said, "Opposition paper, of course."

It had been a statement rather than a question. Billy Vail still nodded. "Granger Reform Party. They hate Republicans, Democrats, and furriners in that order. Naturally they printed what they called an explosion, calling their incumbent sheriff a liar who got fired as a deputy marshal and elected sheriff with a lot of lies about eating cucumbers and doing other wonders long ago and far away."

Longarm muttered dryly, "I think exposé was the word you had in mind, Billy. Either way, it seems an easy problem to solve from here in this easy chair. What's to stop old Walt from just arresting the silly son of a bitch, seeing he's going around claiming to be a wanted outlaw?"

Vail shook his bullet head. "You ain't really been paying attention to your elders. What would you charge a man with if you really felt he'd been killed in a gunfight with the law, say, seven years back?"

Longarm whistled softly. "Yep, seven years *does* take us to the statute of limitations on most charges, albeit not all by a long shot. There's no statute of limitations saying a man can't be tried for murder after seven years, and I'd hate to have to explain a single silver certificate I'd made seven years ago to the Treasury Department, but . . . Just what *were* the charges we had on those Plowright boys way back when, Boss?"

Vail grimaced. "Federal? Robbery. I don't remember.

12

Something to do with postal money orders and government bonds. Like I said, we close the books on *dead* federal wants. Seeing they never got to stand trial, there could be some charges on file in some damned file in some damned basement. Do you really figure Judge Dickerson down the hall would want to preside at the trial of three dead brothers, if and when any federal prosecutor who gave a shit rounded up any witnesses still to be found at this late date? Lord only knows how old those warrants were when I heard those rascals had been seen around Julesberg and sent you boys up yonder to see if they really were!"

Longarm started to make another suggestion another lawman in a jam was in no position to hear. Flicking more ashes in his hat, he sighed and asked, "What does old Walt Wallward want us to do for him, Boss?"

Vail said, "It's stupid. It's too wild for me to justify to the taxpayers of These United States. I couldn't send you up there as a paid-up deputy even if I *wasn't* worried about the opposition papers having a field day with the very notion!"

Longarm insisted, "Very notion of what, Billy? I have some leave time coming to me, and my railroading pals are always happy to offer me and my gun hand a free ride up along the Front Range to the gold fields up Montana way."

Vail hesitated, shrugged, and handed the typed letter across the desk to Longarm. "It's up to you then, on your own time. Old Walt is afraid to force a showdown or just leave the menacing cuss be, as things now stand. Like yourself, he suspects personal enemies may be trying to rattle him into moving foolishly. But contrariwise, there have been cases of lunatics convinced they were somebody more important, returned from the grave or wherever important dead folks come back from."

Longarm started to ask a dumb question. Then he nodded. "Walt wants somebody else who could say for sure to back

13

his play when he exposes this Montana menace either as a political prankster or a possibly dangerous lunatic. You reckon you could spare me for, say, this coming fortnight, Boss?"

Vail nodded. "Long as it's on your own time. But didn't I hear you say something to Henry the other day about that Harvest Moon Cotillion coming up?"

To which Longarm could only soberly reply, "Reckon I'll just have to miss it, but hell, what are old friends for?"

Chapter 2

President Hayes was such an old fuss that they didn't serve hard liquor at the White House these days, and even deputy marshals were expected to report for work in suits and ties. But seeing he'd be on his own unpaid time for the next two weeks, Longarm changed to a more comfortable summer-weight outfit of faded denim with a neatly knotted navy blue bandanna in place of the shoestring tie they liked him to wear at sit-down suppers and such.

He packed a few changes of socks and underwear in his saddlebags, and booted his Winchester '73 to his old McClellan saddle just to be safe instead of sorry should his vacation involve more riding than anticipated. Then he toted his clumsy but not too heavy load on over to the Burlington yards. Sure enough, the dispatcher he'd bought a few drinks for at the nearby Black Cat fixed him up with a free ride north aboard the caboose of a way freight serving stops along the way to Helena.

The railroaders who knew the Big Sky Country of old still called the town Last Chance Gulch, for nothing up that way was all that old to white folks. A French Canadian breed had reported color in a Montana creek as early as '52, but the climate and local Indians had discouraged a serious search until, during the war in the East, some draft dodgers made the first big strike at Grasshopper Creek.

Alder Gulch had been richer, spawning the gold camp of Virginia City that greenhorns still confused with the bigger one out Nevada way. Helena had happened where a party of discouraged prospectors, headed back to the States after searching in vain for even fool's gold, decided to pan the creek they'd camped by just to give the blasted foothills of the Shining Mountains one last chance.

The official production figures since tallied around a hundred and fifty million dollars worth of placer alone. Lord only knows how much high-grade had been pocketed or how much hardrock still remained in the roots of the purple mountains looming over the new capital of Montana Territory.

They'd had to declare a territory, under provisions of the old Northwest Ordinances, after enough settlers moved in to require some government. They wouldn't get to be a state, though, until they had a more reasonable number of registered voters. So meanwhile, Montana was sort of run by a federal administration appointed by Washington, with the more populous townships and incorporated counties allowed to elect their own local governments. The more cautious travelers savvied how informal this arrangement could be out on open range between the more law-abiding parts. The lawmen of Montana Territory—federal, local, or vigilance committee—had their work cut out for them as the combination of gold, land, and water for the taking attracted the sorts who took what they could by hook or by crook.

Once they'd declared Last Chance Gulch their new capital, the still fairly young old-timers had decided the place required a more seemly name. Local legend would have it that Helena won out over a dozen others because it at least had some Hell in it. Others said Helena, Minnesota, had been the home town of one of the original prospectors who'd panned Last Chance Creek. That left nearby Mount Helena unaccounted for unless, as others said, the mountain had been named for the town.

Longarm didn't care. His pokey way freight got him into town well after dark hungry, thirsty, and glad as hell he hadn't wound up with all that fly ash on his best suit.

First things coming first, he toted his loaded-down saddle over to the main street, still called Last Chance, and checked in for the night at the Blackfoot Palace Hotel. For even had he felt like a six-hour star-lit ride across strange range on a strange mount, he knew better than to operate in another federal district, even on his own, without paying a courtesy call first on Billy Vail's opposite number up this way.

They charged him a whole six bits for a corner room with cross ventilation but no running water. He cleaned up as best he could in the gents' bath down the hall, then wiped his gritty saddle down with a damp towel and left it over the foot of his brass bedstead to dry in the thin night air of the high dry town.

Helena sprawled across what seemed a mile-deep valley just above the muddy Missouri, but in point of fact, like Denver, the whole place was higher in the sky than it looked before you tried to run a mile or boil a three-minute egg. But Longarm was used to the altitude in Denver, which even higher. So he was starting to feel springy again by the time he'd put away some corned beef and cabbage with mince pie and two extra cups of black coffee at the beanery across from his hotel.

The Federal Building would be closed at this hour. And he felt no call to compare notes with the town law, since he didn't mean to stay in Helena itself longer than it took a man to ride on out in the morning.

It took him a whole scuttle of beer at the Lucky Seven Saloon down Last Chance to sense he'd made a tactical error in assuming it would have been a useless bother to drop in on the town marshal. The error appeared to be somewhere in its early twenties, dressed more like a dude's notion of a cowhand than a cowhand's notion of a cowhand. A grown man still had to take a kid in fringed buckskin seriously when he was packing a Merwin & Hulbert .45 in a tie-down side-draw rig. So Longarm didn't laugh when the wild-looking rascal demanded, "Ain't that ugly brown hat you're wearing squashed Colorado-style, stranger?"

Longarm nodded pleasantly, considering, and said, "I ain't a stranger. I answer to Custis, Custis Long, and my hat's worn Colorado because I work in Colorado now."

"That's a lie," the truculent side-draw flatly stated. "You ain't working in Colorado now. This here's Montana. So answer my damn question and quit beating about the damned bushes when a white man talks to you polite. Are you some sort of breed? You look dark enough to be part Injun or, hell, nigger now that I'm close enough to smell you."

Longarm put his beer scuttle down on the zinc-topped bar and got his cross-draw clear of the bar with a casual step to his right as someone farther off muttered, "Oh, shit, now he's done it."

But Longarm was hardly in the habit of gunning mean-mouthing fools for fun or profit. So he calmly replied, "I'd be proud to take you up on your kind offer if I knew what this was all about, pard. I sure hope you don't have me mixed up with somebody you're at feud with. I know I've never seen *you* before and I'm good at recalling faces. In the meanwhile, like I just said, I ain't from around here and we've never met before, so why don't we start all over with me buying the next round?"

18

The buckskin-clad but not very comical troublemaker had his gun hand hovering like a hummingbird near the ivory grips of his .45 as he almost purred, "I don't drink with niggers. I don't even tolerate 'em in the same taproom with me. So why don't you just haul ass while there's still time, nigger?"

Longarm knew better than to proclaim his obvious Anglo-Saxon kith and kin as far back as anyone in his family had ever bothered to ask. A troublemaker willing to insult a fairly new J. B. Stetson and call any man of any ancestry a nigger was obviously not interested in any reasonable reply to his wild ravings. The only question remaining was whether he was a hired gun with a specific target in mind or just a fool kid who likely had a mother or, worse yet, brothers.

Since the soft answer had failed to turn away wrath, if that was wrath and not a half-ass excuse, Longarm just smiled thinly and held his thoughts to himself as the buckskin-clad *buscadero* moved his own spurred boot heels wider and announced, "I just told you I didn't want you in here, nigger. But I'll tell you what I'm going to do. I'm going to count to ten before I draw. That'll give you exactly ten seconds to depart these premises or go for your own gun and make it an even dozen for this child!"

Longarm didn't answer. The serious-looking stranger started counting, slow but deliberate. Longarm figured he'd have to make his own move on the count of eight. The morons who played this game usually drew on their own count of nine. But then, just as the boy in buckskin got to six and Longarm's legs were commencing to tense up, the batwing doors from the street swung inward and a loud voice bellowed, "For God's sake, Dakota, don't you know who you were fixing to get shot by? I want both you boys to cut the shit this instant, on pain of any survivors being arrested for premeditated foolishness!"

Dakota, if that was the troublemaker's name, snapped, "Stay out of this, Clinkers. It's a fair fight betwixt me and this uppity coon from Colorado, hear?"

Longarm knew better than to turn his eyes from an armed man who seemed annoyed with him. But he could see the badge on the vest of the older gent in the doorway who was wearing his six-gun high and holding his sawed-off Greener low but handy as he declared in a tone of pure disgust, "You got the *state* right, you fool kid. After that the man's a deputy federal marshal with a High Plains tan. It's a good thing your pal Santee had sense enough to fetch me before you could get your fool self killed. Don't you know who you decided to pick on this time, Dakota?"

The taproom bully stared uncertainly at Longarm and blustered, "Aw, he don't look so tough to me. But you say he's a lawman, Clinkers?"

Longarm felt his ears burning as the older and wiser local told the whole infernal saloon, "He's Custis Long, better known as Longarm, and when he told Soapy Smith to leave Denver, Soapy left. You still want to count to ten with him, Dakota?"

Dakota blanched and said, "Shit, no. I was figuring to draw when I got to nine."

Longarm said, not unkindly, "I know. I don't think you'd have got past eight. I'll be leaving now. Feel free to say you ran me out if that's your pleasure, Dakota. Just don't make any sudden moves as I pick up my change and back out of such an uncouth place. I'd be obliged if nobody else in here twitches one muscle till they've seen the last of me, hear?"

But the older man called Clinkers followed after him, and since Clinkers was wearing that badge, Longarm didn't feel free to draw on him, and said so once they were both outside on the plank walk.

Clinkers said, "Let's go over to my office and drink more sedate, Longarm. I got a jar of white lightning, filed under C for Corn, and we can cut it with some branch water whilst you tell me what in the hell you're doing here in Helena."

Longarm apologized for not having dropped by sooner as the two of them strode up Last Chance to the town lockup. Business had been slow this far from payday. So a kid deputy was keeping a casual eye on the handful of vagrants and drunks in the back as Clinkers led Longarm into a side office, sat him down near a cluttered rolltop desk, and produced the promised jar of hundred-and-fifty-proof along with a couple of tumblers and a ewer of tepid but tangy water.

Clinkers said he'd confiscated the white lightning from an Indian trader. Longarm agreed anyone who offered a Blackfoot a hundred and fifty proof, uncut with enough tobacco juice and gunpowder to make a Quill Indian sick before it could work him up to murderous, was doubtless new at the game. When he asked about Dakota and his more sensible pal Santee, Clinkers explained that both the one Longarm had tangled with and the smarter one who'd recognized him had hailed from the Sioux country further east, or said they had. When Clinkers allowed he'd had trouble with the two of them in the past and wasn't sure what they did for a living, Longarm suggested, "I'd find out if I wore your badge, Clinkers. With Montana Territory so young, it ain't as if there's an endless choice of employment out this way. I've yet to see this Santee jasper. But Dakota was dressed more cow than gold sluice. I take it you're still placer-mining up this way?"

Clinkers nodded. "Far as I know. Some few old boys have took to sinking coyote shafts farther up in the hills, and I hear they've struck silver now down to the southwest at this big lonesome butte. They're hardrocking down *that* way, I reckon. Why do you ask?"

Longarm sipped, grimaced, and poured a tad more branch water in his tumbler as he replied, "I've been through the new settlement they call Butte, imaginative as can be. It's over sixty miles from here and we're talking a gun-toter dressed cow. On the other hand, it's a work night and any working cowhands would be getting up at the crack of dawn . . . where?"

Clinkers blinked, thought, nodded, and said, "I follow your drift now that you've pointed that out. Ain't but a handful of truck farms, butter and eggs, or beef operations within an easy ride of that Lucky Seven Saloon them boys spend so much time in. We're a mite far from the wholesale markets for anyone not serving the gold field towns direct with fresh produce. We do have one brewery over in the foothills rendering snow-melt and local barley malt to not bad suds. I doubt Dakota or Santee do *that* for a living either. Santee is the cooler of the two. He was the one as came here earlier to warn me you was in town, about to gun his foolish sidekick. Dakota is too hot-tempered to be a professional gambler. That leaves us with a pair of what, hired guns?"

Longarm sipped as he considered. Then he shrugged and said, "I thought of that when Dakota first started up with me. In all modesty, hired guns have been hired to stop me in the past. But Dakota falls apart as the real McCoy. To start with, a professional would know he'd never get away with a trumped-up tale of self-defense after he'd been lucky enough to win a fair fight with another trained gunslick."

Clinkers nodded soberly. "He could have back-shot you and lit out, for all the difference it would make at his trial if he failed to get away clean."

Longarm said, "Exactly. I didn't know he was there. I still don't know what his sidekick looks like. So either one of 'em could have just blown me away on their way out the door.

22

That would have to have all that bullshit about counting to ten beat."

Clinkers suggested, "Santee wouldn't have had to say shit if he'd had it in for *either* of you. By the way, he's a tad taller and older, dressed a mite less Buffalo Bill but still sort of old-timey. He went to some trouble and took a chance on making Dakota sore at him by dashing over here to tell us about the trouble brewing in the Lucky Seven."

Longarm decided, "Maybe the older and wiser one's not afraid of Dakota. Sticking to what we know for certain, Dakota picked a fight with me for no apparent reason. Then his pal broke it up before anyone could get hurt. Can you come up with any possible profit in such unreasonable behavior?"

Clinkers sipped at his own tumbler. "I don't even know who they work for, and since you first brung it up, I've been sitting here thinking about all the drinking money those two boys have spent since they drifted in here with no visible means about a month ago. What if we was to arrest 'em on vagrancy and make 'em tell us what they did for a living?"

Longarm shook his head wistfully. "We can't. I'd have no authority in any case, since vagrancy is not a federal offense."

When Clinkers declared he was not federal, by Jesus, and started to rise, Longarm soothingly explained, "You're still bound by that sometimes annoying Bill of Rights. The Supreme Court in Washington has so far allowed individual countries and townships to enact their own vagrancy codes, within reason. But you can't just call a man a bum and lock him up without probable cause. The last I heard, if a man just passing through says he's unemployed but looking for work, you can't put him on your county work gang unless he's flat-ass broke and hence likely to starve or steal in the mighty near future."

Clinkers complained, "You mean I can't arrest me a damned old bum if he's got the price of a damned old sandwich on him?"

Longarm shrugged. "You could likely make less than a day's wages, or less than a dollar to his name, hold up in court. But I don't see how you could hold an old boy with real drinking money on him, as long as he didn't drink too much of it. You'd know better than me how disgusting Helena allows its drunks to get before you pick 'em up to sleep it off."

Clinkers brightened. "By Jimmies! Dakota *must* have been dangerously drunk, to behave so dangerous with a man of your rep, Longarm! What say we arrest him on that and sweat some information out of him!"

Longarm shook his head. "I decline to press charges, and it wasn't you he was threatening. Before you cloud up and rain all over me, I got to get it on down the river far as Wolverine come morning. So I wouldn't be in town when the judge heard their tale about just having a little fun with a new boy in town."

That inspired Clinkers to ask what might be going on in Wolverine, distinguished mostly by a stage stop, a coyote shaft that hadn't produced any color, and a so-called county courthouse for the rare occasions the circuit judge passed through.

Longarm explained, "It's the sheriff of that budding county I'm off to see in the morning. Sheriff Walt Wallward and me used to ride together out of Denver. Do you know him, Marshal?"

The Helena town law shook his head. "Just by rep. Might have met him when he came to town now and again, but if I did we never got past a shake and a howdy. They say he's all right, though. Stomped out a vigilance committee and still busted up the stock stealing down that way with a couple of good arrests. Ain't he the old boy who shot it out with some famous gang one time and nailed five or six of 'em?"

Longarm sipped. "The three Plowright boys, Thomas, James, and Robert. I reckon they were famous enough at the time. Walt tells us now a jasper claiming to be Tall Tom Plowright has been up this way acting odd, though. Might you have heard anything along those lines?"

The older lawman shook his head casually, blinked thoughtfully, and demanded, "Hold on there. Didn't you just tell me your old pal, Sheriff Wallward, shot Thomas Plowright dead? What's he doing up and about if he's supposed to be dead?"

Longarm smiled crookedly. "I told you he seemed to be acting odd. The cuss is someone who looks like him, of course. I suspect I put at least one round in the real Tall Tom myself, and I was there when they lowered him into the ground at Julesberg seven years ago, as dead as a turd in a milk bucket and already starting to turn disgusting. So spare me the speculation about his not being killed after all. I'd rather go with somebody else who just looks like the late Tall Tom. I had this asshole pretending to be *me* not long ago up Durango way. Caused a hell of a lot of confusion when somebody back-shot him and his corpse was identified as mine for a spell."

He set the half-drained tumbler aside as he elaborated. "The hell of it was, the cuss didn't have to look that much like me to worry my own friends a mite. Exact doubles are rare. But heaps of folks look sort of like one another. Did you ever read that *Tale of Two Cities* by Mister Dickens?"

When Clinkers confessed he hadn't, Longarm said, "You ought to. He's a good writer. Slicker than some, who'd have gents who ain't even related look like identical twins. Mister Dickens has this noble drunk change places with a married-up cuss about to have his head chopped off by French rebels.

The tricky part I liked was that the noble English drunk out to save the man of the lady he secretly loves don't look anything at all like the respectable Frog he has to save. He only has to get inside the prison with a pass from some rebel leader, sell the condemned husband some shit, and send him home to his pretty young wife with the same pass, taking his place amidst the prisoners."

"That," declared Clinkers firmly, "was one sloppy way to run a death house!"

But Longarm insisted, "Not really. The pass admitting exactly one gent on official business described what he looked like. But dark hair is dark hair and a man around thirty is a man around thirty, which gets him out the front gate looking *sort* of like the man who went in a while back, see?"

Clinkers said, "I do now. I reckon it could work, if a famous writer says it would. Now that you mention it, I heard about that time Monte Matt Gray almost got buried as the famous Longarm by pure accident."

Longarm pointed out, "Not by *pure* accident. Monte Matt was on the run after a shootout in Leadville. Hearing others had noticed his slight resemblance to me, he tried pretending to be me over Durango way. It didn't work when kith and kin of the man he'd shot caught up with him. They knew who they were gunning. The only confusion, for a time, was caused by his having signed into his hotel in Durango as me. It got cleared up *poco tiempo* as soon as some pals from Denver came to claim my remains. After they got done laughing they went after the killers of my half-ass double. Don't ever claim self-defense in any Colorado court after you've emptied a six-gun into a man's spine on a dark street."

Clinkers nodded. "That never worked for the cockeyed rascal who back-shot Hickok neither. Getting back to here and now, though, you're saying this jasper claiming to be Tall Tom Plowright has to be somebody else?"

Longarm shrugged. "Far be it from me to argue with the Good Book, but had I been there and seen Lazarus or Miss Tabitha up and about seven years after their funerals, I'd have bet more on a close resemblance than a miracle. Tall Tom was fly-blown and part decomposed after an autopsy, and I fail to see why such a worthless crook would rate a miracle even if such things were possible these days."

The older lawman nodded. "I like a ringer just pretending to be Tall Tom too. But why do you reckon the cuss would be out to sell his fool self as a dead outlaw?"

"Just *loco en la cabeza,* most likely," Longarm replied with a weary smile. "You know how many Napoleons and John the Baptists wander in some nights when the moon is full and another tent preacher has passed through during a spell of summer lightning."

Clinkers nodded. "Let me get this straight. You're on your way to Wolverine, Montana Territory, to carry a lunatic back to Denver with you?"

Longarm laughed. "Nope. Ain't sure just what my old pal Walt wants me to help him do about the menacing cuss. Menacing's a hell of a charge to make stick, even when it's on the local books."

Clinkers blinked and declared, "I don't recall such a charge on *my* list of Helena city ordinances, Longarm. Just what in tarnation constitutes a case of menacing?"

Longarm grimaced and said, "I wish you hadn't asked that. I'm not sure of the answer. Menacing is one of those slippery words like, say, indecency or disrespect. We all know what they mean until we try to prove 'em in court. You menace somebody by, well, making them feel menaced. I reckon it would make me feel odd, at least, if some cuss I shot it out with seven years ago took to just sort of hanging about the

Denver Federal Building or the Parthenon Saloon."

"Doing what?" asked Clinkers.

To which Longarm could only reply, "Doing anything at all, damn it. I reckon I'd like it better if some cuss I'd killed in the war started up with a barmaid or started busting up the place. For that would let me kill him some more, or arrest him leastways. I don't know what I'd do if he just hung about the neighborhood, doing nothing but sort of menacing me."

Then he brightened. "Sure I do. I'd send for an old pal who'd been there the first time I killed the son of a bitch. Then I'd get that pal to confirm or deny whether it was the same cuss or not."

"What would you do then?" asked the older lawman.

Longarm started to say something dumb. Then he smiled. "There you go asking questions I can't answer again. I can tell you without looking that the Tall Tom Plowright menacing folks down in Wolverine can't be the Tall Tom Plowright I saw dead and buried seven years ago in Julesberg. After that, I ain't so sure. How do you handle your average Napoleon here in Montana Territory?"

Clinkers shrugged. "You mean one who ain't fired a whiff of grapeshot down the street? What *can* you do but haul him before the judge, who may or may not remand him for a sanity hearing depending on how unsettling he's been acting."

Longarm decided he needed the rest of that drink after all. He picked up the tumbler, muttering, "Right. Like I said, you may know it when you see it, but how do you prove a harmless-acting loon is out to menace anybody?"

Having agreed it was a caution, they both rose and Clinkers walked Longarm out front, where they shook hands and parted friendly. By now it seemed late enough and he'd had enough to drink. So he ambled on up Last Chance to his hotel.

As an experienced traveler Longarm had naturally held on to his room key, so he didn't have to stop by the desk. But the night clerk called out to him anyway, saying, "A gent was just in here asking about you, Mister Long. Said he might be back later."

Longarm glanced at the Regulator Brand wall clock above the key rack. "I sure hope not. I aim to catch me some well-deserved sleep. Did he give you his name? What did he look like?"

The clerk nodded brightly. "He said he was an old friend from Julesberg and that he'd just heard you were in town. He said to just tell you Tom had been by. He said you'd know who he was."

Longarm felt a big gray cat get up and turn around at least three times in his stomach despite the transparency of the fraud as he quietly asked, "Tall drink of water, lantern jaw, and mustache a tad bushier than mine?"

The clerk answered innocently, "That's him to a T. He said you'd know him once I mentioned his name. You forgot the scar, though. He had this white scar just over one bushy eyebrow, remember?"

Longarm said, "I do now. Right eye, you say?"

"I think it was the left one," the clerk replied.

Longarm had been afraid of that when he'd asked the trick question. He swallowed hard, and was mildly surprised by his own calm tone as he quietly said, "If he comes back, send him right on up."

Then he went on upstairs, paying no attention to the way that big gray cat kept swishing its fool fuzzy tail down in his stomach.

Up in his room, he began by moving the bedstead broadside to the doorway. Then he removed the mattress and spring frame to improvise a small fort for his bedroll, spread on the rug between the window and the bedstead's sturdy

29

brass frame. A bullet fired through those door panels would have to twang its way between the steel bedsprings before losing any speed it still had in the cheap and hence sturdy cotton stuffing of the upturned mattress.

He braced a bentwood chair under the knob of the locked door, and seated his heavy army saddle there as well to make a forced entry even noisier if not more difficult.

Then, fully dressed in case he wanted to chase any son of a bitch down Last Chance, he lay atop the covers of his bedroll with his six-gun and Winchester handy and his double derringer on the rug right by his head. Then he closed his eyes and a million years passed slowly while he told himself over and over, "Nothing is going to happen. You don't spook a man and then come calling on him in the middle of the night when you know damned well he packs three guns!"

The son of a bitch had stopped in, knowing he'd be out, with the deliberate intent of making him feel menaced, and so far it was working just as planned, God damn his obvious tactics!

Chapter 3

The morning fog was lifting at Malvern Hill, but he could tell it was going to be another stinking-hot summer day in the Tidewater country and, Jesus H. Christ, how long was this battle supposed to last after all the ammunition both sides had expended in six or seven days of almost constant skirmishing?

Some old boy had been moaning out there in the dark all night, closer than all the others, but it was quiet now as the rising sun burned off the fog to expose the bodies, all those bodies, scattered like rag dolls of blue and gray as the fog let you see ever further and further across the rolling battlefield to . . . Christ, was there no end to them and some still moved, like garden slugs caught out in the open by the sunrise and how many more would die if somebody somewhere didn't call a halt to this insanity long enough to get at least the wounded in off that widespread field of death? Only nobody did and now the movement out there seemed to be hogs, stray hogs off nearby shattered farms, rooting the torn Union blue and butternut gray out of the way to get at the dead bloated flesh of men swollen up like obscene rubber balloons that sounded like big wet farts when they finally burst or a hog tusked into them. And then that first one he'd killed in that orchard was sitting up and staring at him accusingly and he was saying how sorry he was only what was a boy he'd killed at Shiloh doing here at Malvern Hill months later and how could he be accusing anybody of anything after he was killed in another battle entirely?

Longarm stared at the boy he'd killed at Shiloh and demanded, "You think you saw the elephant at Shiloh, boy? We just lost more killed and wounded, on both sides, than they managed in *all* the fool battles of this fool war, *including* Shiloh, up till now! That sissy fight we had last April was nothing next to these last seven days betwixt Mechanicsville and Malvern Hill. If you'll look behind you you'll see fifty-five hundred of 'em down here at Malvern Hill alone!"

The boy he'd killed at Shiloh quietly asked, "How do you know all this, West Virginia? Have you been counting each man as he fell since first you put me on the ground in Tennessee?"

Longarm snorted and said, "I hardy remember how many I've had to kill personal. It's been mighty tedious as well as morose. I read up on the casualty figures later. After it was over and I had time to study more on what I'd been so scared about, see?"

The pallid corpse said, "Not hardly. If you read about all this after the war was over, what are we doing in this fool war?"

It was a good question. So Longarm woke up, repressed a shudder, and told the sunbeams streaming through the window above his little fort on the floor, "I never would have dreamed about a boy I killed fair and square coming back to haunt me like that if I hadn't had other haunts on my mind when I dropped off. I suspect a dead mouse somewhere behind the baseboard accounted for those battlefield smells too. Dead critter is dead critter. The smell of dead mankind

32

gets to us worse because we don't cotton to our kith and kin, or ourselves, winding up like that."

He rolled closer to the wall, sniffed again, and decided, "Could have just been some sloppy eater spilling beef gravy in the floor cracks. Dreams magnify a piss hard-on to a frustrating night in a Turkish harem when you ain't been getting enough lately."

He rolled to his feet and sheepishly put the bedstead back together. Then he put all the furniture back in place, strapped on his .44–40, and enjoyed a good crap and cold shower before he tidied up a mite more, put on his hat and denim jacket, locked up, and went to see if anyone would sell a hungry man some buckwheats with plenty of butter and sorghum syrup in this town.

The beanery across the way served fresh eggs off a nearby farm as well. So Longarm was feeling less menaced by the time he checked in at the Federal Building, only to be told the only lawmen there who outranked him were off chasing road agents again. U.S. marshals got to do that more in parts of the country where the U.S. mails still rode the same coach lines the miners used to ship bullion. Robbing a bullion shipment meant for a U.S. mint was federal too.

Young Henry's older but no wiser opposite number in Helena had nothing on file that Longarm could use. Longarm still offered him a cheroot, and they jawed enough to see they both knew about Sheriff Wallward's odd worries to about the same extent, which wasn't much. So Longarm asked the clerk to tell the marshal he'd be down around Wolverine if anybody in Helena cared.

Getting there was more complicated than just saying you wanted to go there. Helena lay above the Great Falls of the Missouri, and boating on the upper river was a mighty occasional pastime. The town of Wolverine sprawled along a creek of the same name that fed into the upper Missouri

33

from the Big Belts, a spur of the Rockies cutting Helena and the upper Missouri off from the High Plains over to the east. A narrow-gauge serving the gold fields ran down along the wrong side of the Missouri. But Longarm wanted something that beat walking once he got there. So he toted his saddle and possibles over to the Last Chance Livery and hired himself two ponies. The lame old cuss who ran the livery swore both brutes were part cayuse but trail-broke and notorious for their loving natures. So Longarm saddled the cordovan mare with his McClellan, and both horses acted sensible till they thought they had him at their mercy a good walk out of town.

Longarm enjoyed a joke as much as anyone. So after the cordovan crashed through a grove of second-growth aspen with him, bucking and busting up saplings all the way, he kept whipping her across her eyes with his hat and heeling her floating ribs till long after she wanted to quit flying. Then, once he couldn't get her to buck no matter how hard he tried, he ran her downhill toward the river they all had to cross in any case. It would have been easier on her if the roan gelding had wanted to come along. Longarm figured it would do *that* mule-headed son of a bitch some good to skate along the gravel on his dug-in steel shoes with a strong man yanking the lead line sort of viciously.

This only went on for an hour and a half. Once he'd half drowned the two of them, fording the upper Missouri where it ran deeper just to show he meant what he said about staying on the damned trail unless he said different, that loving nature the old liveryman had mentioned began to evidence itself. So Longarm tethered them side by side in a clump of lodgepole pine, and changed saddles to see if the gelding was interested in bucking. But the gelding wasn't. His neck was already sore enough. So Longarm found he could handle them both now with a firm but gentle hand.

Both his survey map and that letter from Walt Wallward allowed it was half a day's ride from Helena to Wolverine. So seeing he had the time, Longarm swung upslope from the official trail to double back, dismount, and slither up a hogback with his saddle gun to see if he had anyone following him. From up there, the trail he'd been following ran like butcher's twine through the riverside timber thinned by the enterprising lads who peddled firewood to the cookstoves and steam boilers of Helena. This far out they'd only cut the good stuff, and left a lot of fast-burning pine and almost fireproof aspen. Longarm was about to slide back down when he spotted dust to the north. He waited till, sure enough, a bitty bright green dot seemed to be riding a black ant along that string down yonder.

Staring harder, Longarm decided it was a gal in a green habit on a black pony sidesaddle. He didn't feel so menaced. It was a public thoroughfare, after all, and the gal in the green riding outfit had timed it about right if she was aiming to make Wolverine that afternoon. He still let her ride on by and kept an eye on the deserted trail behind her till he was sure nobody was following either of them close enough to matter.

He went back down through the trees to his ponies, mounted up, and rode on at an easy angle to the trail till they finally wound up on it some more. From time to time he'd spot a fresh horse apple in the dust ahead. That gal fed her mount genuine oats instead of the cheaper cracked corn or barley most folks in the high country settled for. He wondered if she was pretty as well as rich. He wondered why in blue blazes he was always wondering how to get rid of a gal or what the next one would be like. He hadn't come all the way up here to chase after skirts of any color. That gal in green was just as likely headed somewhere else, and he'd never find out what she looked like in any case. So what did it matter whether she was lonesome or not?

He reined his roan in sheepishly and muttered, "Easy does it. We ain't close enough yet to tear into Wolverine all lathered. If she's headed there, we'll find out just as well the easy way. If she ain't, it won't matter whether we loped or not, see?"

Neither pony argued the point. Now that they were pals, he broke trail once an hour and let them graze a mite. Watering was no problem up here in the headwaters of the Missouri. The trail crossed rills of mountain runoff, great and small, every mile or so.

He was tempted to forge on, knowing they weren't far away from Wolverine, when both the overhead sun and his pocket watch agreed it was high noon. But he didn't want to ride in as others were sitting down to their dinner tables or miss his own noon meal. So he turned off the trail where it crossed an inviting glade of blue-eyed grass to enjoy a shady sit-down under the elm-like hackberry trees at the high end.

He tethered the ponies to graze, and opened cans of pork and beans and tomato preserves as he sat in the onion-scented blue-eyed grass. The tomato preserves would wash down the pork and beans good enough. So he felt no call to waste time building a coffee fire.

He didn't mean to light a cheroot till after he'd eaten. So how come, he wondered, he was smelling smoke?

He went on eating and sniffing till he was certain. Then he wet a finger and held it up to the noon air. A slight coolness told him such wind as there was seemed to be drifting through the scattered trees from the south. So he muttered, "Helena. Lots of cook stoves must be sending up a lot of woodsmoke down that way and we ain't rode all that far."

He finished the last of his tomato preserves, flattened both cans, and drove them under the sod with a boot heel as he reached for that cheroot. Then he sniffed thoughtfully, got back to his feet with the cheroot still nested in a breast pocket, and moved over to the roan to slide his Winchester from its boot, muttering, "I don't know what makes me so curious either. I swear I run in more circles to find out less than anyone I know!"

Then he levered a round in the chamber and eased up into the taller timber to glide silent as a deer through the dappled shade, stopping now and again to test the wind as that odor of burning wood and fresh coffee got ever stronger.

He spotted the horses tethered among the trees ahead first. There was a brown and white paint, a chestnut, and a more recently curried black Morgan wearing a sidesaddle. So Longarm circled, got a thicker screen of thorn-apple scrub between himself and that clearing the smoke was coming from, and eased in for a look-see.

He could hear voices before he could see all that much. A female voice was saying conversationally, "You gentlemen are never going to see a plugged nickel from my Uncle Silas. I don't know who told you he was rich, but even if he was, that shrew he married after my dear Aunt Lorna died wouldn't let him part with a penny just to get *me* back. That woman hates me down to the bone and the feeling is mutual!"

A jovially gruff male voice replied, "Aw, that's all right, Miss Bathsheba. Me and Lefty here don't hate your pretty little bones."

Another male voice, not as jovial, declared, "What are we waiting for, Ike? We all agree she's pretty, and it won't make no difference to her kin whether they get her back screwed or not screwed, will it?"

The one called Ike said, "It's early yet. We won't know till old Piney gets back whether her kin mean to play square with us or not. There'll be time enough for the three of us to screw her if nobody calls the law on us. But if she's right about that muley old battle-ax loving money more than step-kin, we may have to do some riding."

Lefty asked, "Can we screw her first?"

Ike replied calmly, "Might not be time. For all his bull, Sheriff Wallward is a serious tracker. If things don't go as planned, we'd best just cut her pretty throat and light out across that slickrock we already picked out up the slope."

Their obvious kidnap victim sounded close to the edge but trying to stay calm as she asked, "What point would there be in killing me with the law closing in, sir? Can't you see it would go harder for you if they captured you after you'd mistreated me in any way?"

Lefty jeered, "We ain't going to mistreat you. We're going to screw you good!"

Ike chuckled fondly and explained, "He's young and still thinking with his pecker, Miss Bathsheba. My less romantic plans ain't meant in any cruel way. It's just that I don't cotton to spending the rest of of this whole century in prison, and you know who we are. It would've been dumb to kidnap a gal from town we didn't know. How could a man set ransom demands for a gal he didn't know?"

She replied, "That's true, Ike, but if we all knew one another in town before you waylaid me this morning . . . oh. I see."

Longarm did too. By now he'd had time to ponder the pros and cons of waiting for that third member of the gang. The gal was in danger every minute she spent in the hands of such half-witted overambitious extorionists, and he'd just heard them all agree she knew all three of them from town.

The trouble with thorn apple was the thorns. Longarm thought he'd cleared the damned sticker brush as he followed the muzzle of his old Winchester through the narrow gap beween the thorn apple and some box-elder saplings.

38

But just as his eyes met the startled gaze of an auburn-haired gal hogtied in a seated position on the far side of the fire, his damned right sleeve got snagged by a thorn-apple branch and the sound of clawed denim, or perhaps the look in their captive's hazel eyes, inspired the rascals who'd been sharing a fallen log with their backs to him to roll either way, one going for his left-handed side-draw Remington-Rider as the other one tried to whirl all the way round with the Spencer repeater he'd been holding across his knees.

Longarm shot him first, up the ass and then halfway up his spine as it arched in agony. Longarm yelled, "Freeze!" as the other sprawled on one side with that Remington-Rider in his left hand. When the moron just kept moving, Longarm froze him good with a rifle round that blew half his skull away with his black wool hat and more brains than one might have expected.

The gal was screaming mindlessly as she lay on her own side with her wrists lashed to her ankles and fighting the bonds hard.

Longarm moved around the fire. "Calm down, I'm the law," he said as he reached a free hand into his jeans and got out his pocket knife to hunker down beside her.

"Don't cut me!" she pleaded, gasping. "Screw me if you have to but please don't *cut* me, sir!"

He laid his Winchester aside on the leaf litter to firmly grasp the large wriggling bindings as he warned, "Hold still or I might *really* cut you—Miss Bathsheba, was it?"

She sobbed, "Bathsheba Mullens, and I'll do anything you say if you won't kill me!"

He said, "I suspect you ain't been paying attention, Miss Bathsheba. It's over. I'm the law and you've been saved. Nobody's going to hurt you now. Hold still and . . . There you go. Rub your wrists and wiggle your toes inside your boots to get some circulation going before we haul you up on your feet."

She sat up, staring at him more sensibly now as she marveled, "My hands and feet feel all pins and needles. How did you know they were so numb? I hadn't noticed until just now!"

He explained, "You were in no position to think clear, ma'am. I knew how far along the trail you were ahead of me. So I knew they had to have grabbed you minutes before I came along, never noticed, and lucky for you, stopped just down the way to eat my own noon grub. It takes less time than they had you hogtied so tight to go numb like that. Like I said, you were lucky. They didn't know what they were doing. I hate to hurry you, ma'am. But mention was made of a third kidnapper and you just now saw how silly they could act."

As he rose with her and his Winchester, Bathsheba Mullens got a better look at the two sprawled bodies and gasped, "Oh, we have to hide before Piney Woodford gets back. He's ever so mean and . . ."

"I think foolish was the word you were groping for, ma'am," Longarm said as he gently led her to her tethered black Morgan. She seemed to have all her wits back now, and she declined his silent offer of a boost and swung herself lightly up on her uncertain perch. A gal who could mount sidesaddle without help or even a stepping block was a gal who knew which end of a pony the shit fell out of.

As he untethered her reins and handed them to her he explained, "My own ponies ain't far through the trees, and once we get you out of any pending cross-fire I can be sort of mean too, if I have to."

As he led the way afoot, she asked about the ponies they seemed to be leaving behind. Longarm scored that in her favor as well. Then he explained, "We're going to have to send a buckboard party out from town for the bodies in any case. Meanwhile, I don't want empty saddles running home to alert that Piney cuss till I've a better handle on where he might be. Are you sure just the three of 'em were in on it, Miss Bathsheba?"

She said she was, and had him about convinced by the time the two of them were mounted up and ghosting through the trees together, off trail lest they startle anyone with her bright green dress and auburn hair. Her hair was down about her shoulders now, and she had no idea where the veiled derby she'd had on might have landed when the three of them had waylaid her. She'd been riding at a trot sidesaddle, and been roped from the far side and yanked backwards over and off. So he could see how a lady could lose track of her headgear, being dragged and hogtied with her wind knocked out of her a spell.

She described her attackers as recently fired cowhands off one of the modest spreads near Wolverine. He didn't ask how such surly morons might have gotten themselves fired. He wanted her to tell him more about Miss Bathsheba Mullens, and how come those saddle bums had figured her kin might pay enough ransom for her to matter.

That was when she confessed she'd fibbed a mite. Her Uncle Silas owned and published the only newspaper in Wolverine. He and his second wife, Miss Sadie, had brought her out West and taken her under both their wings when her widowed mother, the sister of Uncle Silas, had died a few years back in Iowa. So her Aunt Sadie by marriage had had no call to hate anybody's bones and was, in truth, just swell. Bathsheba had been trying to save money being wasted by telling her abductors they weren't going to get anything for her. She'd seen right off they'd have to kill her either way. Longarm told her she was a mighty brave gal, managing not to get hysterical till towards the end.

41

She blushed and looked away as she was reminded of some of the things she might have said as he was looming over her with a knife. Neither one of them said anything. They both knew what she'd offered. Longarm figured she hadn't really meant it.

To change the subject he told her more about himself, and asked what she'd heard about Sheriff Walt Wallward or anybody menacing him from way back when.

Bathsheba made a wry face and sounded sure as she declared, "Oh, that old windbag is always bragging about his wild career as a U.S. marshal. Uncle Silas says he's what the head doctors call a passionate liar."

Longarm suggested, "I think your uncle means pathological. There are such liars. I've met some. They can't stop telling whoppers even when they know you know they're telling whoppers. Old Walt Wallward had his problems when we rode together years ago, but I never caught him saying anything impossible. And for the record, he *was* a deputy U.S. marshal, senior grade. We were both riding for U.S. Marshal Billy Vail of the Denver District Court at the time I'm speaking of."

She sounded sincerely surprised. "Really? Well, I never. Uncle Silas has challenged Sheriff Wallward in print to show anyone in the county, from either party, his badge and identification or, failing that, his discharge papers from the Justice Department."

Longarm didn't think old Walt would want the niece of an overt political enemy hearing how he'd been fired by Billy Vail, but a man had to try, so he did. "It was over half a dozen years ago, and it ain't as if they give you parchment paper suitable for framing if you just up and quit. But I can back old Walt's story and I got my own badge and identification on me, if you think your uncle would like to see 'em."

She laughed and declared, "I may take you up on that. Uncle Silas is surely going to headline my rescue and all you did for me back there, Custis."

Then she looked stricken and said, "Oh, dear, how awful, seeing you're a friend of Sheriff Wallward! We're opposing his re-election this fall, and you're not going to say you were acting as his deputy just now, are you?"

He had to laugh as he followed her drift. She looked so worried he said, "I wasn't even acting as Billy Vail's deputy, if the truth be told entire, Miss Bathsheba. As I just told you, I'm up here on my own time to look into those reports about Tall Tom Plowright and his miraculous rebirth. Has your uncle printed anything about that in his opposition paper?"

She smiled and confided, "Uncle Silas can write as amusing as Mark Twain when he's inspired. He had a lot of fun with our famous sheriff marching an unarmed newcomer to Wolverine before Justice Steiner on the unusual charge of being alive. After our J.P. told our sheriff not to be so silly, Mister Plowright made a formal statement to the press. He freely admitted he'd been called Tall Tom and might have gotten in with bad company in his younger days. But he defied anyone to produce any warrants or a record of one conviction for any crime, and said he had no idea where Sheriff Wallward had gotten the notion they'd had a famous gunfight in Julesberg, Colorado. He said he was from Ohio before he came out here to pan for placer."

Longarm asked if the man from Ohio could be a tad taller than he was, with a bushier mustache, a lantern jaw, and a scar over his left eyebrow.

She said she'd never been introduced to Mister Plowright, so she couldn't say about that scar. But she'd seen him in town often enough to say Longarm had described him fairly close. She said she'd heard he had a placer claim up

Wolverine Creek, but she didn't know why he seemed to spend so much time in town.

Longarm said, "I'll ask him. There's a lot I mean to ask such an amusing cuss if ever I meet up with him, ma'am."

Chapter 4

The settlement that sprawled up both sides of Wolverine Creek seemed quiet, even for a trail town in the middle of the work week, as Longarm and the gal he'd just rescued rode in. Her uncle's newspaper office and quarters, like most everything else of importance, faced Main Street, a rutted wagon way along the north side of the creek. It didn't matter. In dry weather, Wolverine Creek ran fetlock-shallow in the braided channel it had carved eight feet deep in wetter times. The trail from Helena ran through thoughtful cuts dug by the locals who'd likely filled the deeper ruts with ash and gravel.

As they rode up the far side, Longarm noticed some of the frame buildings facing Main Street and the creek were sort of rustic. The ones made of milled lumber instead of logs tended to be painted, mostly that sort of mustard shade that stood up to the moody climate without costing all that much. As they approached a one-story false front a more yellow shade of mustard, Bathsheba called to the folks clustered on the plank walk out front and they sure yelled back a heap. Longarm had already noticed the fancy lettering across the false front above them proclaiming, "WOLVERINE FREE PRESS."

Before they could rein in, a spry old white-headed cuss with a sort of family resemblance to those elves Rip Van Winkle had been drinking with scampered out into the street to declare, "Praise the Lord, you had us worried, child! That shiftless Piney Woodford came to us with a wild and woolly story about you being held for ransom by that Ike and Lefty he used to work with on the Circle Bar!"

Longarm wasn't surprised when she introduced the elf as her Uncle Silas, and told everyone there Longarm was the hero who'd saved her after shooting it out with the vicious outlaws.

Before Uncle Silas could haul him inside for an interview, Longarm backed his ponies clear of the welcoming throng of at least a dozen folks, raising his voice to declare, "I ain't got time to be in your next edition. Got to call on the sheriff and tell him about two on the ground with one to go. They were more saddle bums than a gang of serious outlaws, by the way."

"They were going to kill me, and worse!" Bathsheba insisted as she gracefully dismounted. "At least come in for some coffee and cake while we thank you properly, Custis."

Keeping a firm grip on his reins and the roan's lead line, Longarm replied, "I'll come back later if you want. Like I said, one of 'em is still at large and . . . you didn't give him any ransom, did you, Mister Mullens?"

Uncle Silas seemed oddly cheerful as he replied, "I had to. He said they'd kill our Sheba if I didn't. So I told him to stay here while I ran up to the bank, and he did, the fool kid. Now we got our local vigilance committee hot on his trail. I sure wish you'd come inside so we could discuss it better in private."

Longarm said, "Later," and whirled his mount to head on up the wagon way, scanning building signs till he spotted the one he had in mind. He reined in out front as a familiar figure stepped out of the sheriff's office to ask, "What's all that commotion about down the way, Custis? I was just fixing to come down and ask when I spied that Colorado crush. I'd forgot how tall you were, but I can't say you've changed that much, old son."

"Neither have you," Longarm lied as he dismounted but hung on to the reins and lead line. It wouldn't have been polite to tell a reformed drunk he looked somewhat older but far less dissipated these days. That drinking problem he'd had years before had apparently been even worse than anyone had guessed. Old Walt's hair and mustache were grayer, but his leaner and healthier features had a much better color now. Longarm said, "We ain't got time to compliment one another, Walt. Silas Mullens just consulted your friendly neighborhood vigilance committee on a serious family matter. We'd best get you possed up and I'll tell you about it along the way."

The older man wearing a fancy shirt and gilt badge gasped, "Damn it to hell, I told Lester Kenmore what I'd do the next time he hosted an informal necktie party! My remuda's out back. Don't need no posse to deal with Kenmore and his half-ass night riders! Follow me!"

Longarm did so by dismounting and leading his two jaded ponies after the sheriff afoot. They passed through a breezeway between Wallward's stoutly built log lockup and a frame shop next door as Longarm called out, "I could use a fresh mount for me and this rig as well, Walt. The three of us left Helena sort of early this morning."

He saw the eight or ten head of riding stock corralled out back as Wallward replied, "Pick one out whilst I get my saddle and throw rope from the back porch, old son. That high-stepping barb with a diamond blaze ain't broke to gunfire yet."

Longarm settled on a steady-looking bay mare, and the older man roped a bigger black gelding for himself while Longarm brought him up to date on the kidnapping of Bathsheba Mullens in as few short sentences as possible.

As they were getting the bridles and saddles aboard the mounts they'd picked, Walt observed, "Old Silas got word to someone on that infernal vigilance committee as he was taking the ransom money out of the bank. You're right about those three saddle tramps being stupid. I've had all three in my drunk tank overnight more than once. If you and the Mullens girl were expecting Piney Woodford to return to their coffee fire with the money, I reckon Lester Kenmore could. Lester may not be a college professor, but that Piney Woodford is *really* stupid, if he's still alive."

Longarm cinched his McClellan securely and led the bay mare clear of the splintery corral poles to mount her as he suggested, "We might be able to head 'em off. I know the way bee-style, whilst an old boy riding back from town with money might zigzag some in hopes of hiding his trail."

The sheriff swung himself abroad the bigger bronc as a window on the far side of the corral swung open and an older but not bad-looking gal called out to them. Longarm savvied the sheriff's living quarters lay back yonder when the older man yelled back, "Haven't time to talk about it, Flo! This here's the junior deputy I told you about and the two of us got some serious riding to do!"

His woman, housekeeper, or whatever called something out about the roast in her oven. Wallford yelled for her to go ahead, and assured her they'd be back in time for supper as he led the way back to the main street through another opening in the store fronts facing the creek.

They didn't ride down Main Street. The rider who knew the country better led Longarm directly down the steeper bank up this way, and they splashed across to heel their fresh

48

mounts up as scary a climb on the far side. They punched through the more spread-out buildings on the south bank, and headed up the logged-over south slope of the valley. Then Wallward suggested, "You'd best take the lead from here, Custis. You say you figure a furlong off in the trees from the trail to Helena?"

Longarm nodded and replied, "We'd do best running a contour line even higher and then easing down toward that camp. The survivor will surely bolt for some slickrock his pals mentioned when he finds them dead. But that might not be all bad—for us. We're both fair trackers, and we sure don't want those vigilantes cutting Piney's trail before we can!"

Then he reined in a quarter of the way up the open slope and pointed. "Aw, shit, they already did."

The older lawman said something worse than shit as the two of them rode west through the tree stumps toward the triumphant group of two dozen riders, returning with the three they were bringing in riding facedown across their own ponies. Walt Wallward grunted that the one on the checked shirt was Piney Woodford. He'd apparently been riding a paint pony as well.

As they rode closer, the sheriff told Longarm, or warned him, that the hungry-looking rider in the black frock coat and matching flat-brimmed hat was Lester Kenmore, owner of the Three Triple Seven beef spread and self-anointed avenger of misdeeds.

Longarm muttered, "Didn't those vigilantes who did so much to discourage claim jumping in these parts a few years ago sign their death threats with a three, followed by three sevens?"

The sheriff said, "They did. I told Lester to cut that shit when I was elected to keep the peace in these parts more constitutional."

As if he'd sensed they were talking about him, the darkly dressed rider on the dishwater gray pony called out, "Howdy, Sheriff. Look what we found over on Thornapple Hill. These lunatics kidnapped Miss Bathsheba Mullens and then tried to make a stand of it when we trailed Piney here back to their hideout."

As Longarm and the older lawman fell in with the ragged column on its way back down the slope, Longarm quietly said, "I hope you don't expect to see things that way in the *Wolverine Free Press*, Mister Kenmore. Because it ain't the way it happened."

Kenmore's eyes narrowed a tad, and his voice was not as friendly when he quietly asked, "Who's this stranger who just now called me a liar, Sheriff?"

Wallward sounded jollier as he replied, "He ain't no stranger. He's an old boy I broke in as a lawman down Colorado way. You may have heard of him. They call him Longarm, and I wouldn't call him a liar neither."

Before things could get worse Longarm explained. "You and your pals had already ridden out when I carried Miss Bathsheba home, Mister Kenmore. But she was there as a witness when I had to gun Lefty and Ike. I'll take your word one of you must have gunned Piney there. I never laid eyes on him till just now."

Kenmore grumbled, "Well, shit, I never said anybody shot anybody formal. What I *meant* to say was that we trailed Piney Woodford back to his hideout, called out for anyone there to surrender, and seeing they never answered, fired at will till the silence from the other side inspired us to move in cautious and find the three of 'em down."

Longarm let it go. He was just as glad the older lawman with him didn't see fit to ask why none of the outlaw's ponies had been hit in such a fusillade, or comment on how lucky it was that Miss Bathsheba had already parted company from her abductors before all that blind firing. Nobody ever told the truth about a vigilante execution. It hardly seemed likely anyone was going to really care how three such worthless saddle bums had wound up dead. Dead saddle bums were an improvement over most any alternative, once you studied on it.

The hitherto drowsy little town perked up considerably as the vigilantes rode in to place the three bodies on display, propped up on planks in front of the *Wolverine Free Press*. You couldn't have drawn a bigger crowd with a public hanging and free lemonade.

Longarm took advantage of his being an outsider to drift his mount on back to the sheriff's office and tether it out back, still saddled in the unlikely even he might have sudden need for it. Then he drifted back to the other end of Main Street to rejoin the fringes of the crowd. He kept his mouth shut and his ears open as the various rival bullfrogs of the bitty puddle debated the best ways to dispose of three shiftless skunks. It appeared another older gent in a rusty black suit was the bemused Justice Steiner, with no more authority than a local justice of the peace rated under common law. Longarm was glad to see old Steiner didn't take himself as seriously as some small-town J.P.s did. His appointed position gave him the authority to enforce town ordinances, issue licenses, marry up the unwary, and so on. He had to remand any serious cases to the fully qualified circuit judge who served a whole mess of towns in those parts in turn. But as Longarm listened, Justice Steiner proclaimed the only serious crime that anyone had committed under his jurisdiction had been the abduction of Miss Bathsheba Mullens. So the criminals who's done it, being dead, could hardly be put on trial. He added that their deaths were a matter for a coroner's jury to decide on. Another older man they called "Doc" announced he'd gather some of his usual pals and they could hold their session as usual in the Big Belt Saloon up the way after supper time so everybody interested in giving a statement could drink on a full stomach.

Longarm was about to speak up about his own willingness to tell his tale to the panel when his eyes met those of another face in the crowd. That face rose a head taller than any around it, and as Longarm digested that lantern jaw, the bushy mustache, and the scar over the bushy left eyebrow, that big gray cat began to stir in his guts some more.

The disturbingly familiar figure crawfished back through those around him as Longarm elbowed his way toward it. By the time Longarm had bulled out the far side of the crowd, the tall drink of water he sure thought he'd seen the last of years before was walking off, not looking back. Like Longarm, the somewhat taller man was wearing denim work duds and a cross-draw gunbelt. Bathsheba Mullens had said Walt Wallward had brought him before Justice Steiner unarmed. If so, he'd picked up a big old Patterson Colt Conversion since then.

Longarm was muttering, "All right, it looks like him, but it ain't," when the man with the uncanny resemblance vanished into a narrow slot between two buildings. Longarm broke into a trot and drew his .44–40 as he ducked into the same slot.

It was empty. He whipped on through to the alley just in time to see his quarry circle an alley shithouse to enter a back door.

Longarm followed his gun muzzle down the alley and through the same rear entrance to find himself in a narrow hallway. He eased to the archway at the far end. When he spied an old geezer and a young squirt playing dominoes on a corner table, he savvied it was a saloon. Old boys hardly ever played dominoes that calmly in company with drawn guns. But Longarm kept his six-gun out anyway. Then he took a deep breath and stepped out into the taproom.

He lowered the muzzle more politely down his right leg when he saw Tall Tom, if that was Tall Tom, bellied up to the otherwise unoccupied bar. The fat bald barkeep shot Longarm a thoughtful look, then went on wiping glasses behind the mahogany as Longarm reholstered on the way over. He bellied up beside the somewhat taller man, told the barkeep he'd have the same, and quietly told the man next to him that the night clerk in Helena had mentioned an old friend who was looking for him.

The taller man stared down at his beer schooner as he replied in a laconic tone, "I never said we were pals, Longarm. They say it was you as killed my kid brother Bob."

That seemed to inspire the two domino players to vacate the table across the otherwise deserted taproom. As they were leaving Longarm replied just as calmly, "I told a wanted man called Bob Plowright to put his hands up. He chose to die instead. His brothers, Jim and Tall Tom, were shot up in the same display of stupidity. It was seven years ago and the face was puffier as well as all blotchy, but I can see how a more superstitious soul could take you for the tall one. Would you care to tell me who you really are in the name of the law now?"

The uncanny resemblance picked up his beer with his gun hand as he calmly replied, "My name is Thomas Plowright. Folks back home in Ohio used to call me Tall Tom because I was so short. I've already had this dumb conversation with other lawmen. I wanted a word with you the other night when I heard you'd come up from Denver to horn in. I know my kid brothers done wrong. I've gotten over the desire for revenge I'll allow I felt at the time. For I'd warned them time and time again that the wages of sin are death."

Longarm left his own gun hand right where it was as the barkeep slid another schooner his way. As the mysterious stranger sipped in an annoyingly enjoyable way, Longarm said, "All right. I'll go along with your silly game. Assuming you somehow got back up after collecting your wages down Julesberg way, what *did* you want from me if it ain't revenge?"

Tall Tom, as he called himself, put down his drink to calmly explain, "I wanted to ask you to talk some sense to Sheriff Wallward. He keeps telling folks he killed me seven years ago. Lord only knows where he got such a notion. They say he used to drink more than he should have."

Longarm said, "I can tell you where he got the notion. I was there and Walt Wallward was sober enough at the time. If it wasn't you he pumped full of lead it sure was . . . Hold on, might you have had another brother? Say an identical twin?"

The man who certainly looked like the late Tall Tom shook his head wistfully and said, "Nope. There were three of us—poor Bob, Jim, and myself. You'd know better than the rest of the family how they went wrong out Colorado way. I wasn't with them when they got in trouble with the law, praise the Lord."

Longarm was dying for a sip of that beer. He reached for a smoke with his left hand instead. "You're good. I can see how you spooked old Walt with his sinister innocence. I'm supposed to ask how come you were killed alongside your brothers if you claim you weren't there, right?"

The taller man murmured, "Ask anything you like. I've nothing to hide. I've papers to prove who I am, and everyone who seems to know me from the past agrees I'm me as well. Why are you lawmen harassing me this way? Is it because Sheriff Wallward's running for re-election this fall and you want everyone to remember his earlier fame riding as a federal lawman?"

Longarm made a wry face and replied, "The political rivals you're working for would know who's out to harass whom. Let's see all that identification you've been bragging about, if you're Tom Plowright."

"Do you have a warrant saying I have to?" asked the tall stranger.

Longarm said, "Not hardly. Feel free to write your congressman as soon as you recover, if you want us to do this the unfriendly way."

The tall stranger addressed the worried-looking barkeep as he slowly raised his own left hand, declaring, "You're my witness that I'm only going for a billfold now, Stubs."

The barkeep, who seemed to know him, murmured, "This ain't my fight, Mister Plowright."

The man he'd so addressed drew a pigskin billfold from an inside pocket of his denim jacket, and placed it before Longarm atop the bar as he suggested, "Read 'em and weep."

Longarm lit the cheroot between his teeth by thumbnailing a match head with his left hand and getting rid of the match before that same left hand pulled out a library card, an Ohio voter's registration, and a folded-up Montana mining claim from a compartment of the billfold. He spread them like playing cards to read. He then said, "I reckon I could go to Illinois and sign up to vote or even take out books as James Butler Hickok, if I was of a mind to spook folks and recalled where he'd originated."

He blew a more thoughtful smoke ring at the spread-out mining claim and mildly asked, "You panning much color up the creek?"

When the taller man grudgingly allowed he hadn't struck gold so far, Longarm muttered, "I ain't so astounded, seeing I heard earlier prospectors coyoted all the way to bedrock alongside the same creek without hitting shit. You just happened to decide to pan for color up the creek from a sheriff who shot it out with you and your brothers seven years ago, right?"

The taller man shrugged. "Gold is where you find it. I'm doing nothing unlawful anywhere. As to shooting it out with anyone, my brothers may have been there. Do you really think I was killed in that same gunfight?"

Longarm shoved the billfold and papers toward their owner as he replied in a disgusted tone, "Not hardly. We both know you're a paid imposter. There'd be no profit in anyone putting on this dumb act on his own, and you don't strike me as a lunatic convinced he's somebody famous. Tall Tom Plowright would be a long-dead and long-forgotten road agent if you and the rascals you're fronting for hadn't chosen to evoke his memory so brazenly."

"Who do you suggest I'm fronting for?" asked the brazen bastard as he put his papers back in his billfold in an annoyingly unhurried way.

Longarm said, "I ain't playing. Schoolkids used to play that game with me when I was still young enough to go along with that I-know-something-you-don't-know bullshit. You ain't going to rattle me into doing anything stupid."

Sheriff Wallward came tearing through the swinging doors with his Schofield out, demanding, "What's going on in here? What's Tall Tom trying to pull now, Custis?"

Longarm sighed and said, "He's trying to make us look stupid. So put that stupid gun away before you wind up in the newspapers again, Walt. I was just telling our tall friend here how it wasn't going to work."

The older lawman lowered his gun muzzle, but didn't re-holster his old thumb-buster as he licked his lips and asked, "Don't you agree he's Tall Tom or the spitting image, Custis?"

Longarm said, "Hell, none of us look exactly the same as we did seven years ago, and we only saw Tall Tom on the fly when he was alive. The real Tall Tom is dead and buried. That's a fact. I've been trying to get this asshole to tell me who he really is and what he's really up to, but as you found out earlier, he's a brass-balled son of a bitch they must have paid good after choosing well!"

The man insisting he was a dead and buried outlaw turned to the barkeep to state in an injured tone, "You're my witness the two of them have been waving guns at me and calling me cruel names. I don't have to stand for being called a son of a bitch, and there's no shame in refusing a fight at two-to-one odds, so I'll be leaving now, and you know who to go to if they gun me on my peaceful way home!"

He snapped a coin on the bar next to his half-drained schooner, and Longarm snapped, "Let him, Walt!" as the taller man turned away to stride grandly out the front door. When the sheriff took a hesitant step after him Longarm quietly said, "Don't. They want you to. Can't you see it?"

The older lawman turned to him, looking mighty puzzled, as he replied, "Not hardly. That damned Tall Tom has been fixing to drive me back to drink ever since he showed up with that sneaky smile and purring answers to perfectly sensible questions!"

Longarm took a deep swig of suds—it was about time—and stuck the cheroot back between his smiling teeth before he replied. "That too. Anyone that intent on raking up the past would surely know you used to have a drinking problem, no offense."

He took a drag on his smoke and continued. "Let's agree he's damned and forget about him being the real Tall Tom. Anyone can see how easy that part was. Hell, given the four years you've been sheriff to work with, I could come up with a fair double for you, me, or even Billy Vail, as soon as you consider how many dishonest gents there are in this wicked world and what some of 'em will do to make a buck."

Walt Wallward signaled a beer for himself as he bellied up beside Longarm and speculated, "Suppose it was only a double riding with the Plowright boys that time, and then suppose—"

"Forget it," Longarm said. "Let's stick with Ockham's Razor. William of Ockham was the smart old-timer who passed down the laws of evidence a smart lawman ought to follow. Old Bill said whenever you had a simple solution balanced by a complicated solution, it was safer to go with the simpler one. Two outlaw brothers teaming up with a dead ringer for an older brother who was taking out library books back home in Ohio sounds way more complicated than three bad brothers stopping them stages together. We know what happened when we got word the three of them were spending their ill-gotten gains in a Julesberg house of ill repute. You were there when they buried each and every one of the three of 'em. There were no survivors. What do you want, an egg in your beer?"

Wallward sipped at his plain draft, said it would do fine, then suddenly gasped, "Thunderation! I'm *drinking*! That spooky son of a bitch has me so proddy I clean forgot I'd signed the pledge!"

"You better quit whilst you're ahead then," Longarm suggested as he slid his own beer away. "They've already made you look like a man who believes in haunts, or a lawman who pesters innocent placer miners for no sensible reason. As Stubs here can tell you, the cuss is good at getting himself harassed. I confess I was tempted to pistol-whip him, and I ain't even running for office in these parts!"

"You mean you think someone like that infernal Silas Mullens or Lester Kenmore put that tall drink of water up to all this shit?" the older lawman demanded hopefully.

Longarm shrugged. "You'd know better who your political enemies might be. Ockham's Razor says that makes more sense than dead road agents coming back for a rematch, right?"

Chapter 5

Longarm was glad to see that that thoughtless gulp of soft
liquor had failed to lead a reformed drunk astray by supper
time. Once they'd seen to their ponies, washed up out back,
and gone on upstairs to meet the little lady, Longarm could
see how a man might reform for such a pleasant old gal.

Florence Wallward couldn't have been all that young when
first she'd met the poor cuss she'd saved, but you could see
she'd been a real looker in her day, and she was still a
handsome woman in a gray and motherly way. Longarm
wasn't surprised when her husband bragged on her once
being a stage actress. It wouldn't have been polite to ask a
lady why she limped like that, but old Flo, as she allowed him
to address her, must have been used to folks being curious.
For she was the one who explained right at the supper table
how she and her Walter had met as orphans of the storm,
both down on their luck in a Dallas boarding house, after
she'd been in a train wreck and lost her job with a touring
dramatic outfit.

The supper she whipped up was handsome too. For despite
a sort of dramatic way of talking, old Flo knew real folks
liked real grub, and her pot roast and mashed potatoes tasted

just right after that light canned dinner he'd had much earlier that day.

Over the peach cobbler and genuine Arbuckle coffee she served for dessert, her man got to grumbling some more about Tall Tom Plowright and his menacing ways. So Longarm shot his hostess an apologetic look and said, "Dang it, Walt. The only real menace is what he's got you doing to your own self. That cuss pretending to be Tall Tom is neither a haunt nor a hired gun. He's a stage actor, like Flo here used to be, albeit he's not half as pretty."

The crippled-up former actress blinked in surprise and declared she'd never thought of that. Once she had, she nodded at her husband and said, "I see what Custis means, Walter. As you say in your book, you never got a really good look at any of those wild Plowright boys until they came out shooting, and you, ah, might not have been yourself at their funeral. Say someone recruited a vaguely similar-looking man about the right age and build, got him to grow the same sort of mustache, and then coached him some about the real Tall Tom's past."

"What about that scar over his eye?" asked the sheriff uncertainly.

She dimpled and said, "Heavens, I could manage that with my old makeup kit, Walter. Who's to say that scar is real anyway?"

Longarm said, "William of Ockham, ma'am. I was studying that scar in good light, from closer than I am to you right now. But might it not be more simple if we consider whether the real Tall Tom really had a scar over *either* eyebrow?"

Both older folks stared wide-eyed at him. So he said, "I only my own self *remembered* such a scar, or thought I did, when a room clerk back in Helena mentioned it just last night. It just hit me, as we were speculating over this swell coffee, how it was Walt here, in his letter to Billy Vail, who described the way Tall Tom appeared when he first came to Wolverine. Lord only knows where any old wanted fliers with earlier descriptions of the three of them might be filed these days."

Flo Wallward looked uneasy as she asked, "Are you implying my Walter didn't know what he was saying when he came home white as a sheet to say he'd seen Tall Tom Plowright in town and had to do something about it, crazy as it seemed?"

Longarm said soothingly, "No, ma'am. The cuss in question looks like Tall Tom to me as well. On top of that, he *says* he's Tall Tom. All old William of Ockham and me have to say is that we ought to forget the picky details and go with what we've got for certain."

When her husband asked what they had for certain, Longarm told them both, "A stage actor. A haunt's just silly, and no hired gun would traipse around for weeks putting his intended victim on the prod before he just went *after* him."

"You're frightening me, Custis!" the motherly old gal told him in a sort of quivering tone.

Longarm said, "I'm trying to say there may be less real danger to your man than that stage actor and the sneaks he's working for want us to suspect. Ockham's Razor gives us the coming election as the most likely motive. The most simple way to keep a man from winning any sort of contest would be to simply kill him. Don't blubber up on me, ma'am. Ockham's same logic says that when someone doesn't kill a rival it's because they don't have the nerve. Nobody who'd go to so much trouble could *like* a man too much to have him dry-gulched, and anyone can see how easy it would be to do that to any lawman as he makes his rounds afoot or saddled up."

"You sure paint a cheerful picture," the older lawman sighed.

Longarm said, "I'm trying to. Lester Kenmore just showed us he was capable of killing a man he had the drop on. Is it safe to say he ain't running for sheriff against you come November, Walt?"

The older man at the table shook his head and replied, "I doubt he's that interested in politics. Lester's more a natural bullyboy who gets tired of punching cows from time to time. The Granger Party, inspired by that cussed Silas Mullens, hasn't announced a candidate to run against me yet. But mark my words, they will."

Longarm frowned and asked, "Ain't it sort of late to hold a party convention and select a slate of candidates, Walt?"

The older lawman shrugged. "For all I know they've already done so. You know how the Granger Movement meets almost as secret as the KKK or Red Flag Socializers. Controlling the only paper in the county gives them one hell of an edge on us real Americans."

His wife gently chided, "You shouldn't swear at the table, Walter." But the angry older man said, "Hell, hell, and double-hell. I was here first. But ever since that Silas Mullens started his radical rag, he's been raking me over the coals as an incompetent or worse!"

Longarm allowed there was nothing worse than an incompetent lawman, and asked what else they'd printed about him, aside from seeing ghosts from the past.

The sheriff sighed. "Oh, Lord, would you like it alphabetic or numerous? It's my past the sarcastic cuss keeps casting doubt on in print. You know how some newspaper men glorify everything out this way all out of proportion, whilst others like to call Kit Carson a squaw man and dismiss Red Cloud as a Digger Indian? Well, Silas Mullens is one of them kind. To hear him tell it, Hickok was another worthless drunk who never heard a shot fired in anger, and I never said I was famous as Wild Bill, durn it."

Flo confided, "We sent him a copy of Walter's book when he first began his newspaper a few years ago. He might have simply ignored it if he didn't think it was well written. He didn't have to make fun of my Walter by printing things out of context and implying they were big fibs without offering any proof of his own!"

Longarm asked more about this book she kept citing. Her husband looked embarrassed and said Longarm wouldn't be interested, but she explained, "Walter was writing it when first we met down in Dallas. It was about his recent experiences as a federal lawman, and I found it fascinating. I may have helped him a little with the spelling and grammar. But after we'd tidied that and had it typed up in multiple carbon copies, I was sure we could have it published."

"We couldn't," her husband said. "Everyone we sent it to either thought it was too tame or too wild. Like I said, they either want a Saturday night in Dodge to sound like the Battle of Bull Run or a church picnic. But I'm still glad I took the time to get some things down on paper whilst they were still fresh in my mind. It might have helped me face some ugly truths about myself, even before I met up with Flo here."

"You're in the book, Custis," the motherly Flo softly said with a moist look in her eyes. "You covered for a superior who might not have been himself more than once, didn't you?"

It had been a statement rather than a question. So Longarm didn't have to explain how he'd once felt about a senior deputy who'd been decent, drunk or sober, to a greenhorn trying to learn.

When she asked if he'd like to read a carbon copy of the book he was in, Longarm nodded but said they'd best get that coroner's hearing out of the way first.

Walt Wallward said he'd almost forgotten that fool hearing, and added he was just as glad he wasn't invited, seeing he'd had nothing to say about the kidnapping of Bathsheba Mullens.

Longarm said, "I'm inviting you. You'd better tag along if you're serious about running for re-election this November, Walt."

The sheriff said, "I am, but dang it, nobody ever reported any kidnapping to me to begin with."

Longarm said, "I know. They call that compounding a felony. Let's go lay down some law about that, pard."

When they got to the saloon they were told to go around to the back entrance. They understood why when they saw Bathsheba Mullens and her kin inside. Young ladies of her station were not escorted through public taprooms for any reason if it could possibly be avoided.

There were two round card tables provided for the regulars in the back room of the Big Belt. That evening somebody'd spanned two planks across them to improvise one long hearing table. Some extra chairs had been hauled in to face each other across the bare lumber. The local vet who doubled as county coroner was already seated with his panel. So he told Longarm to have a sit-down next to the other witnesses. Sheriff Wallward wasn't invited. So he moved over to stand against one wall with a dozen others neither called to testify nor forbidden to listen in.

Longarm found himself seated next to Bathsheba, with her uncle and Lester Kenmore on her far side, in that order. Longarm didn't know the three other men further down. The coroner introduced his fellow panelists as a storekeeper, two town aldermen, and a quartet of stockmen who likely had nothing better to do in town that evening.

The coroner called on the kidnap victim to testify first, since she'd been there from the beginning. Longarm listened with approval as the spunky auburn-haired gal demurely told her tale without any needless dramatics or fibs as far as he could tell. He felt a mite awkward when she got to the part about him appearing out of nowhere, firing from the hip, to save her from a fate worse than death. All the old coots on the panel were smiling at him when she added those saddle bums had said they were going to kill her afterwards.

When she'd got to the end of her own tale alive and pure, Longarm declined the invitation to speak next, saying he had nothing to add to a true tale from a lady they all knew and that he was as curious as them about what the other witnesses had to say before he offered his own observations.

So they called on the kidnapped gal's Uncle Silas, who told about the same tale of suckering Piney Woodford into letting him get word to his pals on the vigilance committee. When he said good old Lester and his riders had recovered all the marked silver certificates, the coroner allowed he'd been pretty slick, all right. Then he called on the owner of the Three Triple Seven to wrap the story up.

Longarm listened with interest as the modest hero explained how they'd trailed Piney Woodford back to his hideout in a discreet way, surrounded the small camp, and called upon the desperadoes to surrender. Longarm noticed Lester had changed his tale a tad to fit the testimony of Bathsheba Mullens. There were still a few holes in it, such as the lack of holes in the wad of paper money the late Piney Woodford had been packing in a breast pocket. But Longarm felt no call to pick at scabs that didn't matter. He waited till the riders who'd been in the ferocious gun battle on old Lester's side had had their say. Then, when the coroner declared they'd heard about enough unless someone else had something to add, Longarm nodded and said, "I do indeed, sir. As a lawman of some experience I'd sure like to know why everyone behaved in such a damnfool manner."

He turned politely to the gal beside him. "Forgive the way I had to put that, ma'am. There was no other way to describe a whole mess of grown men who'd put a lady in such needless danger."

Lester Kenmore half rose to demand, "What are you talking about? We had to try and save her when her uncle told us she'd been kidnapped by them desperadoes, didn't we?"

Longarm kept his own voice calmer by far as he answered. "Nope. You had a paid-up sheriff to call on. Coming over here just now, Sheriff Wallward assured me he has four full-time deputies and at least two dozen good men he can posse up in a pinch."

"So he says," sneered Lester. Old Silas Mullens was about to say something more when Longarm rose to his considerable height to announce, "I wasn't finished. Whether the man a majority of the folks in these parts elected could have saved Miss Bathsheba or not is moot. He and his own riders couldn't have done worse had she still been at the mercy of three live saddle bums when you and your vigilantes came at 'em like armed and dangerous schoolboys."

Lester Kenmore rose to his own feet and commenced to sputter like a lit fuse. But the coroner banged on a plank with the butt of a Colt Dragoon and snapped, "Simmer down and let the lawman have his say, Lester. I fear I follow his drift."

Some of the other older and wiser heads were nodding, even before Longarm continued. "If we accept your story at face value, and I've no call to call any man here a liar, Mister Kenmore, you and your boys called upon the kidnappers to surrender and opened fire when your reasonable request was replied to with a pistol shot or more. Might I ask where you thought their *victim* here might have been as you emptied your guns into the woodsmoke and greenery?"

The boss vigilante stared down at Bathsheba Mullens and stammered, "She wasn't there with those saddle bums. Didn't you just hear her say she was with you? Don't you even remember saving her, seeing you bragged before on gunning at least two of the gang?"

Longarm shrugged modestly and said, "Let's not score dead skunks on one another. My point is that you and your riders couldn't have known where the lady was when you opened fire. For all you could have known she was hogtied, sitting up, smack in the middle of camp. As she was when I got her out of there before you could fire a salvo through her pretty head!"

One of the older jury members decided, "He's right. How about that, Lester?"

The boss vigilante flushed red, scuffed at the floor with his boot tip, and blustered, "All right, Piney Woodford came out with his hands up and told us his pals were down and the gal was gone. If you must know, he was shot trying to escape later."

The coroner nodded soberly and asked, "Why didn't you say so? I find all three deaths justifiable homicides, if not suicides. Nobody with a lick of sense would kidnap a gal from around here and let her kin have time to get word to the vigilance committee."

Longarm asked mildly, "Wouldn't it read better if you admonished one and all to call on the proper authorities next time?"

The coroner hesitated, nodded, and said, "Be it so ordered, with no fines or penalties levied on anyone for shooting skunks out of season. Tell the sheriff you're sorry, Lester."

Kenmore protested, "I wasn't the one who come running that his poor innocent niece had been kidnapped, Doc!"

The coroner decided, "You're right. Silas Mullens, tell the sheriff you're sorry."

The newspaper man rose to his own feet, red as a beet, and might have said most anything had not Walt Wallward beaten him to it by graciously announcing, "No apologies are called for, Doc. I'm sure everyone here did what he or she thought best and all's well as ends well, like the Good Book says."

The coroner chuckled and declared, "I suspect it was Shakespeare who said that, Sheriff. But you're right and I declare this hearing over and done with. The Reverend Morrison says he'll be proud to say a few words over the three of 'em after we toss 'em down that coyote shaft we've been meaning to fill in anyways."

So that brought everyone else to their feet, and Longarm found the auburn-headed Bathsheba almost arm-in-arm with him as they headed out the back way. She must have noticed too. She said, "You said you'd come back to let us thank you properly, Custis."

He nodded down at her and murmured, "Meant to. Been tied up with a mess of other matters. Those saddle bums who kidnapped you may not be all the troublemakers left in town. I had to eat supper too."

She insisted, "We'd have given you a fine supper. The evening is young and we'd still be happy to coffee and cake you. You don't have to worry about Lester or his friends making trouble for you or your friends, Custis. He's a big old gruffy bear, but he'll do as I say if I tell him to leave *my* friends alone."

Longarm smiled thinly and replied, "I'm not all that worried about your vigilance committee, Miss Bathsheba. I know you and your uncle find that cuss calling his fool self Tall Tom mighty comical. But *I* think he looks like Thomas Plowright too, and you don't seem to have a Western Union here in Wolverine."

She said, "My friends call me Sheba, and the nearest

Western Union office is in Helena. Were you going to wire somebody about that mysterious Mister Plowright?"

He shrugged and helped her down the back steps in the trickier light out of doors as he explained. "*Somebody* has to be fibbing about gunplay I took part in seven years ago. I need more facts to go with the little I can say for certain. Mayhaps we'll get to talk about it some more if I see you around town before I have to leave."

He couldn't make out her expression in the dim light, but her voice sounded hurt as she replied, "Oh? Sure, maybe we'll see one another around town."

Then she was headed one way with her uncle and their friends, while he and Walt Wallward were crunking alley cinders off in another direction. Longarm wasn't sure just why he felt so morose as the older lawman chortled, "By the Great Horned Spoon you sure shoved it up old Lester's ass and busted it off! You made Silas Mullens look sort of stupid as well, Custis. Maybe now he'll stop calling me a blustering fool in his damned newspaper!"

Longarm said, "I doubt it. But I reckon we scored a few points for proper legal procedure, and small-town gossip can be mightier than the political pen. How come he keeps calling you a blustering anything, Walt? No offense, but I ain't heard you bragging all that much about anything foolish or otherwise."

Wallward confided, "Maybe he's got me whipped down. I told you I let him read that fool autobiography Flo had typed up. It was her idea others might care to read it. I only set down some thoughts on paper as I was trying to pull myself together after Billy Vail handed me the shovel. I was mad enough to kill old Billy at the time. But even then I knew he was doing me a favor. It ain't no kindness to keep a man in drinking money when he shows up drunk for work. It's even worse if the job involves powered machinery or loaded guns."

Longarm nodded soberly as they walked along, but let the older man do the talking. Wallward said, "Flo sent a copy of my fool book over to Silas Mullens when she heard he meant to start his own newspaper here in town. She meant no harm. How was she to know he was a Granger to begin with and a born doubter in any case? You know the first thing the mule-headed cuss gave me a hard time about? He sneered that I was no more a Westerner than he was because I'd allowed in my first pages I'd been born and raised east of the Mississippi like him!"

Longarm snorted, "Like him, Hickok, Custer, and Cody? Hardly any white folks really born out this way have had time to grow all the way up yet. Remind me to assure him the famous if overblown Billy the Kid hails from New York City, while I warn him not to call Luke Short any sort of sissy because he was born in New Jersey. What part of the East did you start out in, Walt? I'm from West-by-God-Virginia myself."

The older man chuckled and said, "I notice that every time you open your mouth. I'm an Indiana boy myself. We had us eighty-five acres of bottomland along the Wabash but I was a younger brother. You'll find it all in my autobiography, Custis. You ain't going to get out of leafing through it at least. Flo asks questions."

So Longarm wasn't surprised, a few minutes later, when the motherly Flo Wallward served them marble cake and hot chocolate in her kitchen and then showed their guest to a feather bed upstairs with a candle in one hand and a manila-bound copy of her husband's famous book in the other.

Once he was alone with it, along with a bed lamp, he found

himself curious about the parts they'd told him he was in. So he got undressed, lit a cheroot, and propped himself up under the patchwork comforter to give it a go.

The neatly typed but poorly written autobiography made for rough going. He couldn't tell whether it had been old Walt or his better educated wife who'd been inspired by the works of Sir Walter Scott, but as in the case of the interminable Waverly novels, the even less interesting tale of Walter Wallward wandered all over without getting to all that many infernal points.

By skimming over a heap of repetition Longarm was able to keep at it. He could see why every publisher they'd ever offered it to had turned it down. But he failed to find the few actual facts too wild to accept, and some of them were sort of interesting to a man who'd been there.

The cases Walt said he'd worked on before Longarm had been with the outfit sounded sensible. He'd heard Billy Vail mention a few of the more outstanding arrests. But Longarm felt sort of silly when he got to the part about his own swearing in as a junior deputy. It seemed that nobody saw himself exactly the way others saw him. Longarm had never considered himself such a ladies' man, and he was certain he'd never felt that much puppy-dog devotion to old Walt as his junior. He'd have done as much for anyone he wasn't sore at, as long as it was no skin off his own ass. What kind of a kiss-ass would tell the boss another worker hadn't shown up yet because he was too drunk to rise and shine?

Old Walt had been facing some truths indeed when he'd been putting things like that down in black and white. Longarm wasn't so certain a man running for public office would want to admit right out what a self-deluding drunk he'd been before he'd seen the light. But a lot of reformed sinners were like that. Longarm chuckled, turning a page, as he was reminded of that old joke about the sinner at a revival meeting going on and on about all the gals he'd fornicated with, until the preacher had to warn him he'd gotten past confessing into bragging.

The carbon-copied and dog-eared pages finally got around to that shootout in Julesberg. Longarm noted with approval how old Walt gave credit where credit was due, and told the tale about the way things had gone. Longarm read over those pages twice to make sure he wasn't skimming over anything. There was nothing about a scar over Tall Tom's dead eyebrow in this original version. So a doubtless worried man had written Billy Vail about that feature he "remembered" after seeing it for the first time on the live face of that menacing stage actor. The rascals who'd recruited a ringer had doubtless known nobody was apt to be dead certain of every detail of a dead man's face, years after thinking they'd seen the last of it.

But that scar could be the loose thread a more doubting lawman could use to unravel the tangled web they'd woven with a similar mustache, maybe some hair dye, and certainly some brass-ball lies.

So Longarm leafed through to where Walt had been fired and set to work on all this self-examination, then put the thin but tedious tome aside, snuffed the lamp, and caught himself some sleep.

The next morning, over bacon and eggs with fried potatoes, he told the elderly couple why he had to send some telegraph wires. Old Walt didn't seem to follow his drift, but his wife, being an old actress, allowed it seemed a fine idea to ask theatrical booking agents as well as other peace officers about unusually tall dark "heavies," as such villainous-looking stage actors were called, who might have a scar over the left eyebrow whether they had bushy mustaches or not.

When Walt Wallward grumbled about the revival of Tall

Tom Plowright not being an infernal stage play, his wife asked, "How do we know that, Walter? As Custis just pointed out, the man wouldn't act so menacing if he was capable of anything worse, and we *know* he can't be the real Thomas Plowright!"

Her husband scowled down at his coffee cup and declared, "I've a good mind to just run him out of town and be done with all this menacing! What could a sissy stage actor do if I was to just tell him to slap leather or saddle up?"

Longarm washed down the last of his breakfast and said, "He could do neither and make you look like a blowhard. No matter who or what he is, he knows no professional peace officer is going to gun him or even pistol-whip him for no good reason. That's why he just purrs at us without doing or saying anything that would give us the excuse to really crack down on him. It don't take much nerve to act the part of a mysterious gun-toter when you know nobody's apt to take you up on it."

Flo dimpled at Longarm and said, "I can give you the names of all the booking agents I ever dealt with in my younger days. But I still find it hard to believe anyone would book a *real* villain from any of the agents I ever got a booking from!"

Longarm nodded. "So would I, ma'am. It's more likely Walt's secret enemies sort of stumbled over or happened to know some full- or part-time stage actor who needed the money. I'm sort of clutching at straws when I say I'll take you up on that offer about booking agents. But it's worth a try. If he is a professional he's a sort of unusual-looking cuss. How many scar-faced stage actors do you reckon there could be standing close to seven feet tall? That was a big fib about him hailing from Ohio too. Walt here already pointed out I talk like West-by-God-Virginia. I'd say that fake Tall Tom started out in the Tidewater country around that Chesapeake

Bay, or just as likely, Upper Canada. He talks like a regular American till he gets to words such as *out*. Then he says *oot* like a Scotchman. Folks around the Chesapeake or Great Lakes do that. Real Scotchmen make lots of other amusing noises."

Flo Wallward nodded to her husband and said, "You were right, dear. This young man is really good! I'd better get cracking with that list of booking agents. Will you be staying overnight in Helena, Custis?"

Longarm said, "Might be able to save me some time, ma'am. Instead of sending heaps of wires and waiting on answers, I thought I'd send one long one to another peace officer I know up to Fort MacLeod."

Walt Wallward, who was paid to keep track of things in his neck of the woods, looked up to ask, "Are you talking about that Mountie post just north of the border?"

Longarm nodded. "That border's closer to us than Denver, and I've worked with Crown Sergeant Foster before. He's a good old boy with a curious nature, and there's an outside chance that menacing cuss down this way started out menacing folks up Canada way, right?"

Chapter 6

Longarm was more than halfway down the creek aboard the cordovan he'd found most responsive to neck-reining and bare-heeling when he heard a familiar hail and turned in the saddle to see that Bathsheba Mullens overtaking him. She'd changed to a more practical tan poplin habit and put her sidesaddle on a dapple gray that morning. Her hair was pinned up under a straw boater. She looked as if she'd put herself together fast as well as casual. He saw why when she fell in beside him to demand, "How dare you leave town without even saying good-bye to me, you mean thing!"

He smiled at her with his free hand tugging his hat brim as he replied, "Wasn't leaving Wolverine entirely yet. Got to send a telegraph message to Fort MacLeod. They have a swell relay station up yonder, and a pal of mine can gather all sorts of information all day and wire it back to me tomorrow, see?"

She didn't seem to care about that part. She quietly asked if she could keep him company up the trail to Helena.

He tried not to leer as he replied, "I never have such luck. I'm only fixing to ride as far as that narrow-gauge across the river. But I sure could use the company if you ain't got nothing better to do."

She said she'd barely gotten to speak to him, let alone thank him after he'd saved her from those ruffians. Then she asked, "How can you wire Canada from just across the river, Custis? There's nothing there in the way of a town, let alone a telegraph office."

He patted one of his saddlebags as he assured her, "Don't need one, if I set my mind to it and shinny up a pole. I've got me this old Signal Corps telegraph key here. Learned the trick in the war, along with Morse Code. Out on patrol, we used to listen in on enemy telegraph messages or even send some fake ones to confound 'em. So I can save us the long ride up to the capital and back by tapping in to the cross-country lines along that railroad track. Neither the railroad nor Western Union likes it much, but they've found it takes less time to feed me a carrying current and relay my fool message than it does to argue with me in Morse."

From other questions she asked along the way, he could tell she neither knew nor cared much about electomagnetic theory or Morse Code. He was glad. She was a pretty little thing and he enjoyed her company, but she was still the niece of a political enemy with a venomous pen and an opposition newspaper to put out.

They chatted their way to where Wolverine Creek fed into the far broader upper Missouri. This far up, the so-called Wide Missouri was a far cry from the big brawling river folks below Great Falls knew. It started out, like other rivers, as an ambitious creek, growing a tad wider and deeper every time it captured another branch brook. Hence the swirling muddy water was only a furlong across where the trailside Wolverine Creek ran into it.

Longarm regarded the swirls thoughtfully as he told his companion, "You'd best sit tight here while I find out whether I'm right or wrong about the gravel swishing down this faster creek in wetter times."

But she said, "Pooh, you keep forgetting you're on my range. I've forded here many a time and you're right about the gravel bar. It's stirrup-deep most of the way with a little deeper drop-off near the far bank."

He said that sounded good enough for him, but he still wanted her to lag back a length in case the bottom had shifted since her earlier passages.

It hadn't. They made it almost without incident. Bathsheba laughed and shouted "Wheee!" as she had to lift her skirts almost to her knees to keep them out of the muddy water while fording that one deeper spot. She didn't seem to have any pantaloons or even stockings on above the tops of her English riding boots.

They forged on up through the spruce and aspen on the unsettled far side of the river. When he asked her what she'd been doing over this way on her own, she said, "Just riding. Haven't you ever just gone riding over a hill to see what lies on the other side, Custis?"

He smiled and said, "Yep. It's usually another hill. But I know the feeling. Is that what you were up to yesterday when I spotted you on the trail almost all the way to Helena?"

She explained she'd actually been to Helena, although she couldn't explain why. She said Helena was almost as boring as Wolverine, and that she surely missed the bright lights and window shops of Sioux City.

He said he knew what she meant. He'd been to Sioux City. It was a county seat, built up before the war with stockyards, pottery ovens, machine shops, and all sorts of interesting stuff.

She said she'd been born there. That made her less than thirty years old. But he'd already figured that out. He had her around her middle twenties. A dangerous age for a single gal with a heap of imagination stuck in a dinky out-of-the-way town.

They got to the single track of narrow gauge, hugging a contour a safe distance above any possible flooding of the river to the east. As Longarm had hoped, a line of larchwood poles carried a double line of wires along the upslope side. Longarm got them well clear of the tracks up that way, and as they dismounted to tether their mounts to aspen saplings he warned her, "This is likely to seem long and tedious to you down here. But don't sit on the ground under aspen anyways."

She assured him she wasn't that much of a city gal. So he didn't worry about her getting covered with ticks as he fished out the gear he'd need to tap the top wire up yonder.

She remained close by, watching with interest as he crimped bare wire to the mousetrap-sized Signal Corps key. She asked, "Don't you need your own electric battery for that thing? A boy back home had this electrical set he'd sent away for and there was this pickle jar of acid that turned his fingertips all brown."

Longarm said, "I've seen those kits they sell bright kids. Western Union uses way bigger battery jars, set up in series so they can give you quite a shock if you don't know what you're doing."

He pointed with his pliers at the wires above. "I know what I'm doing. The railroad sends its signals at lower voltage along the lower line they can get at easier. Western Union's hitched a ride with 'em along that top wire. They keep a current going all the time, and it's the breaks in the current you make with this key that they read up or down the line. When I break in it'll garble things till the operators leave off to see what I have to say. Once we get to talking I'll just ask 'em politely to relay an official government message unless they want the government sore at 'em. I have the same argument with 'em all the time and, so far, I've won."

79

He tucked the key and dangling wires in one hip pocket, put the pliers in another, and got out a couple of yards of pigging string, about the size and softness of clothesline, only tougher.

He moved over to the larchwood pole to loop the pigging string around both the pole and his own rump, muttering, "This would be a mite easier if I had some of them climbing irons the telegraph boys use, but there's a limit to what one man can carry in two saddlebags. I think it was a German general who sat down one time to list all the things a cavalry trooper might find use for in the field."

Then he gripped the splintery larchwood with his hands and knees, leaned most of his weight against the rope loop across his butt, and started inchworming up as he continued. "Old Fred the Great said to forget it as soon as he saw nothing but an elephant could ever carry a trooper and all that stuff. Fred the Great was smart about things like that. He trained his soldiers to make do with what they had as soon as they got where they wanted to go."

Longarm was less afraid of heights than some, but he still found it tough to carry on a conversation as he worked his way ever higher into the Montana sky. The poles running along a contour line so high above the river made it seem even higher, even though he knew there was no way to fall all the way down to the river if he slipped.

There were two other riders down that way, as he could see from up on the pole. They'd reined in where the trailside creek ran into the main stream, as if they were arguing about something.

Longarm stopped climbing. If they looked up this way they'd have a time making out his head against the tree tops all around. His hat brim would shade his face while looking like little more than a bitty brown dot. The range was so great they were little more than dots to *him*,

80

even out in the open on the trail.

Both their ponies were bays. One rider was dressed dark, maybe all in black—like that menacing cuss who said he was Tall Tom? He wasn't sitting tall enough in his saddle.

The other had on a gray hat and a light tan or maybe buckskin shirt. But what was he doing yonder if he was that surly cuss from Helena they'd called Dakota?

Bathsheba called up, "What's wrong? Are you stuck?"

He called down in a quieter tone, "Keep it down to a roar. I ain't stuck. I'm staring at some strange riders across the way. Strange to me, at any rate. Seeing it's your town, Miss Sheba, do you recall a Wolverine rider who favors a bay pony, a buckskin shirt, and a dove-gray hat peaked cavalry-style?"

She called back, "That doesn't sound like anyone I know. On the other hand that's not such an usual way for a cowboy to dress, is it?"

He allowed he guessed not as, across the river, the two strangers seemed to be headed up Helena way. That was sort of interesting when you studied on it. Why would two riders rein in and argue as if they didn't know whether to ride upstream or down, unless they didn't know where they were going, or who they were following?

He let them ride around a bend, out of sight, before he shinnied on up to where the bottom wires almost touched his sling. Then he slung his ass in a more comfortable position and got to work with his pliers. As soon as he'd tapped in to the top line he pocketed the pliers and got out the notes he and the Wallwards had worked out between them after breakfast. Breaking into the telegraph traffic and arguing in Morse with an overly officious division supervisor was so tedious he found himself more interested in that now-deserted trail across the river. The more he studied on those riders, the more that one reminded him of Dakota. But what in thunder would the troublemaker he'd backed down want with him now?

The old border-town bullshit where one cuss started up with you so his pal could throw down on you from behind made no sense after you considered Dakota's pal running to the law that night. Why would two strangers to the territory start up with another stranger, drop it, and then trail him all over the country as if out to . . .

"Menace him," Longarm decided, even as his chattering mousetrap put him in contact with the Northwest Mounted Police at last. You sent messages in Morse far slower than even a dullard got to think, so Longarm found himself thinking about being menaced, even as he asked Fort MacLeod if his old pal, Crown Sergeant Foster, was still stationed there.

They told him Foster was, as he wondered what profit there could be in menacing anyone who wasn't running for any damned office that November. They surely knew making faces at a paid-up federal deputy wasn't the way you got him to lose interest in your case.

Then he forgot those mysterious riders for a spell as he asked the Canadian operator to take down all those questions he'd like Crown Sergeant Foster to look into for him up Canada way. He knew he was taking advantage of a Canadian lawman in asking him to check with all those theatrical booking agencies in the .States. But at least he only asked about the bigger ones west of the Mississippi. Old Flo had pointed out that all aspiring stage actors started with the better-known agencies, and even when the agencies turned down an aspiring Hamlet, they would be inclined to recall scar-faced seven-footers.

He asked the Mounties to check out some other stuff as long as he was up there, and told them where to send the answers in, say, twenty-four hours. Then he detached his tap, repaired such little damage as he'd done up there, and shinnied down to rejoin the auburn-haired gal at the base of the pole.

Bathsheba stopped pacing to declare, "You were right. It was so boring I thought I was going to scream. Do we have to wait here for any more answers, Custis?"

He moved over to the tethered ponies and began putting things away as he told her, "They haven't begun to answer yet. I only saved me a few hours by short-circuiting Western Union like so. I asked them to wire me back in care of the telegraph office up in Helena. I want my answers on paper, and it would *really* be tedious perched up a telephone pole with paper and pencil for Lord only knows how long. They'll wire each answer, care of Western Union, as they get it. I can pick 'em up all at once tomorrow afternoon just by riding on up the river once."

She demurely asked, "When do we start for Helena then?"

He smiled uncertainly and replied, "I just said I don't have to be there for better than twenty-four hours. But before I carry you on home across the river, we'd best make sure nobody's out to pick us off in midstream. Might you know another good ford, say downstream at least a mile and, better yet, offering less cover on the far bank?"

She nodded eagerly and said, "I can do better than that. I know a swell lookout where some say Blackfoot used to watch for strangers out to cross the river either way. It's just down the tracks about a mile and a half. The railroaders had to tunnel through it and the river had to oxbow around it. The change in the current piles a wide shallow ford just downstream and—"

"I'd rather see it than talk about it," Longarm cut in. So the two of them mounted up to ride along the dirt service path beside the tracks until, sure enough, the tracks ahead ran into a cavernous dark tunnel, with the rocks above smudged almost as black by engine smoke.

Bathsheba pointed up through the trackside trees, and led the way up and about until they suddenly burst out in the open again high overhead.

Bathsheba warned, "Be careful of that slickrock!" as they reined in on an acre and a half of sod that was nestled by a ragged horseshoe of wind-polished sandstone.

Longarm allowed he never flew where he could walk as he dismounted to tether to some rabbit bush. Nothing taller could grow in the wind-scooped hollow where bedrock lay so close to the surface.

The girl, who knew the place better, slid from her own saddle to secure her own pony where it could graze the shallow-rooted but lush greenery. She took Longarm by one sleeve, saying, "Come this way. I found this castle in the sky the second summer I was out here. I don't think anyone's been up here since the railroad was built."

He found that easy to buy as she led him over a few yards of bare rock to a smaller grass-filled nest a heart-stopping lurch short of a sheer drop to the brawling brown Missouri's hairpin bend down yonder. She pointed just downstream to a satiny-smooth patch in the current, saying, "There's the ford I told you about."

He glanced across at the lower far shore. Winter flooding had cut the old-growth forest over that way off at the roots. The aspen and alder that had sprung up in the last summer or so couldn't hide much from anyone up here with such a bird's-eye view. He swung his gaze upstream, where those unexplained riders had vanished around a more wooded bend. He decided aloud, "No way they can work back down without our spotting them. I got some baking chocolate and tomato preserves in a saddlebag. What say we sort of picnic here long enough to make sure of those rascals?"

Bathsheba said chocolate and tomatoes sounded divine,

and sank gracefully to the sod as he ambled back to their ponies and broke out their simple but likely ample enough repast.

Baking chocolate wasn't any sweeter than the tomato preserves, but she was a sport about it when he explained he packed it because it carried the kick of chocolate without melting or going rancid on a serious rider. She allowed the tomato juice helped the hard bittersweet chocolate to go down. She already knew chocolate could keep you awake almost as good as coffee, and cut your hunger even better.

As they reclined side by side in the sky, chewing and swallowing, she suddenly blurted out, "Take me with you to Helena tomorrow, Custis!"

He swallowed thoughtfully and softly replied, "I'll only be there a short spell, Miss Sheba. Where I'll be headed from Helena depends on what my pals at Fort MacLeod find out for me. If I don't get any serious charges on that menacing placer miner up your way, I may not be around Wolverine all that long either."

She said, "I don't care. Take me with you when you leave and it won't matter where we end up."

He smiled gently down at her. "It always matters in the end, Miss Sheba. It ain't that I don't follow your drift, and I don't want you to take me for a sissy. But I ain't in the habit of running off with adventuresome small-town gals. I keep meeting up with gals like that in my line of work. You meet 'em all over this country, in other small towns, working as hotel maids, hash house waitresses, or dance hall gals, if they were lucky. The ones I've talked to tell me they can't go back to the small towns they run off from, safe and warm as they may have felt there in more tedious times. it's tough enough for us men to lead adventuresome lives on the open road, Miss Sheba. You don't want to run off with some stranger just passing through. Men and women fight enough

85

when the man has a nice steady job that keeps him at home every night."

She sighed. "I know. I ran off from Sioux City with a traveling man who said he meant to settle down. Maybe he did, later on. You're right about how snug and warm the place you left can seem to you after a few short months following a charming vagabond from one cheap hotel to another. But in my case my mother took me back in when I came crying back as her ruined daughter."

Longarm killed the last of the tomato preserves and reached for a cheroot as he marveled, "Yet you want to run wild some more? After the lesson you surely learned, Miss Sheba?"

She looked away, blushing, as she murmured, "It wasn't the pillar-to-post existence I learned to enjoy. It was the nights, on firm bedsprings or soft. Half the time we ate high on the hog, and other times we lived on hope and bread crusts. But the nights we had together in bed, those lovely nights with our bodies locked together as one and my feeling so happy I really believed all his sweet lies about tomorrow . . ."

"Aw, cut it out, you're making me feel horny," he said as he was trying to get a damned match to light.

Bathsheba lay back across the springy sod, reaching up to unpin her hat and let down her auburn hair as she softly said, "Why don't you *do* something about it then, Custis?"

He put the unlit cheroot away and got rid of his own hat as he muttered, "Well, Lord, nobody here can say I never tried. But I hope you understand you can't elope nowhere else with me, Miss Sheba."

She began to unbutton her tan bodice as she smiled up at him to say, bold as brass, "I never wanted to leave home again, damn it. I've just been dying for some real loving for more than a year now!"

He believed her, once they'd gotten enough duds out of

the way for him to roll between her welcoming bare thighs and discover she hadn't put on any underwear before riding out after him.

She gasped, "Oh, Christ! Yes! It's even bigger than I was hoping for!" as he entered her, gently at first and then, seeing she could not only take it but seemed to want more, driving it all the way in to make her gasp in mingled shock and pleasure as he hit bottom.

She locked her booted ankles around his shirttails and tugged her rumpled skirts up so their bare bellies could grind together as she tried to suck his tongue out by the roots. So it wasn't so long before she was shuddering in orgasm as the head of his old organ-grinder exploded against her wet marshmallow womb way up inside of her twisting torso.

Then, seeing they were old friends, they got all the way undressed for some home-style rutting in the bright sunlight of their grass-lined love nest high above the rolling river.

She couldn't seem to get enough, and kept changing positions in a mighty acrobatic way. Her lovely sunlit body, auburn-haired all over, inspired him to acrobatics as well. But it wouldn't have been romantic to sing that dirty old cow-herding song, even though they *did* seem to be doing it every way but through a bobwire fence.

He didn't comment on at least one fib he'd caught her in either, as she said that had sure been fun but suggested they get really down to some serious pleasure. She'd said earlier she'd been out here for more than a year. Yet she'd complained she hadn't had any of this for just *one* year. That sure was something to contemplate as he watched his love-slicked shaft part her auburn hair dog-style. But he knew a gal was as apt to lie as any man when you asked them who else they'd been screwing lately. So he could only hope she wouldn't tell on *him* when they got back to town.

Chapter 7

They enjoyed every advantage of their vantage point until they felt nobody else was coming. Neither of them felt like coming anymore for a spell. So they got dressed and Longarm took the lead, a round in the chamber of his saddle gun, as they gingerly recrossed the upper Missouri. It hadn't felt so broad crossing the other way.

But nobody was laying for them in the sparse cover on the other side. Nobody tried to ambush them on the trail back to Wolverine. So they rode in trying to look innocent and it must have worked, because nobody called Bathsheba a liar when they dismounted out front of her uncle's newspaper office and she told the old cuss, who'd come out on the steps, how she and Longarm had run into one another a few minutes before just down the trail.

Silas Mullens invited Longarm to come on in and stay a while as he stuck type for the next edition. He said Sheba could fetch them both some beer and pretzels from the quarters out back.

Longarm had naturally dismounted to hand Bathsheba down from her sidesaddle and tether her mount for her. But he told them both he had to get on up to the sheriff's place, having been gone so long, to say whether he'd be there for supper or not.

Silas Mullens insisted, "Tell 'em you're supping with us and I'm serious, old son. Aside from us owing you a good feed for all you've done for Sheba here, we got us some notes to compare on the coming elections. I know you're fond of old Walt Wallward. There's no law against keeping canary birds or mice for pets either. But I'd like to hear more about his distinguished career with real lawmen before I put out the next edition."

Longarm said, "I didn't come up here to engage in politics and I admire the U.S. Constitution. But whilst freedom of the press may be one thing, outright libel is another. You go saying Walt Wallward is a liar who never rode with the U.S. marshal's office and I'll have to appear as a witness against you when he sues you for slander."

Silas Mullens chuckled in an elfin way and said soothingly, "I wouldn't print anything about anybody I can't back up. That's why I was hoping we could have a nice long conversation—over, say, dessert and cigars—about your misspent youth as Walt Wallward's junior deputy, he says."

Longarm ignored the warning looks Bathsheba was sending his way as he scowled at her uncle to growl, "I *did* ride with Walt as his junior deputy, and he showed me some ropes that have saved my bacon a time or two since! The man's an old pal. What kind of a polecat would low-rate an old pal for the finest supper and grandest tobacco on Earth?"

"That's not what I'm asking," the newspaper man insisted with a weary shake of his head. "I said I wanted to check some things out with you. I never said I expected you to bear false witness against anybody. You've already inspired me to reconsider some of the gossip I confess I might have taken at face value just because of our opposing political notions.

89

But you weren't here when Walt made all those grand proclamations about law and order. He fussed at the town council for a gun ordinance, saying card-playing, strong drink, and pistol-packing made for noisy payday nights. But has anyone paid a lick of attention? I could take you over to the Big Belt this minute and show you plenty of young jaspers wearing six-guns this afternoon!"

Longarm nodded soberly and said, "I'll take your word for it. I've been in town a spell. But tell me something else. Did your town council *pass* any gun ordinance at your county sheriff's request?"

The newspaper man smiled sheepishly and said, "Touché. But how much good is a sheriff nobody pays any attention to? Walt's told our Lester Kenmore and the boys what he thinks of their vigilance committee too. But you just saw how scared they were to ride out after Piney Woodford and my marked money when I got word to them about Sheba here being kidnapped."

Longarm snorted in disgust and said, "I thought we agreed last night on how dumb that was. You can't have it both ways, Mister Mullens. You can have an elected sheriff backed up by friends and neighbors, or you can treat him like an unwelcome stranger and wonder why he never seems to arrest somebody nobody has even mentioned to him."

Bathsheba reached out to touch Longarm's sleeve as she pleaded, "Do come to supper, Custis. Aunt Sadie is a grand cook and I promise Uncle Silas here won't try to make you join the Granger Movement."

When he hesitated, she softly added, "I thought maybe we could get to know one another better this evening. We barely got to say more than a few words along the trail just now."

Longarm could only hope her uncle would think he always laughed that silly. He recovered and soberly assured her he'd be proud to get to know her better.

Her uncle seemed oblivious to her blush as he grinned up at Longarm. "My Sadie serves at six sharp. You'd best get back a tad earlier if you mean to set down with clean hands and all your wind, old son."

They shook on it. Longarm ticked his hat brim at Bathsheba, who dimpled demurely as if butter wouldn't melt in her mouth. Then he remounted and rode the short way up to old Walt's lockup.

It seemed everyone in Wolverine watched the main street out their windows. The sheriff came out like a clockwork cuckoo to stare up at Longarm and demand, "How did you ever get to Helena and back so soon? I'd best go tell Flo she didn't put enough spuds in the oven."

Longarm swung down from his McClellan as he replied, "Hold your fire, Walt. I won't be supping with you and Flo this evening, no offense. Only had to ride as far as that telegraph line up and down the big valley. Used the old Signal Corps trick to put some questions out across the land. Got invited to supper at the *Wolverine Free Press* on my way back just now."

Walt Wallward seemed totally confounded. So they went inside to sit and smoke while Longarm brought the older lawman up to date on his recent adventures, leaving out the slap and tickle with the auburn-haired Bathsheba, of course.

Walt said he hadn't noticed any strangers in town earlier, with or without buckskin shirts and dove-gray hats creased army-style.

Longarm said, "I could have been wrong about a tan flannel shirt at that range, and lots of old boys crease their hats the same way. There's no law saying they were the odd lot I ran into the other night in Helena. They could have just been two local riders on their way to most anywhere. Neither one ever shouted across the river that they were trailing anybody."

The older lawman chewed on his stogie like a bone and decided, "You're too good at reading the way others move to be spooked for no good reason. I've a mind to gather a few of the boys, ride on up to that so-called claim, and bring that so-called Tall Tom in for some serious questioning—in the back where sound don't carry."

Longarm took a thoughtful drag on his own smoke and quietly said, "That might not be your very best move, Walt. Like I just told you, I accepted that invite to supper from Silas Mullens with a view to scoring points in your favor. How would it look if you were beating the shit out of a suspect while I was trying to convince him you were an old pro?"

The older lawman snorted, "Nothing you can do or say is going to make Silas Mullens print nice things about me, and I wasn't talking about questioning anybody Ranger-style, damn it. Due process allows us to run somebody in on *suspicion,* and nobody can say that son of a bitch ain't been acting suspicious. What if we was to salt him away for the usual seventy-two hours on an open booking, and meantime let him know we were expecting some answers to all them wires in way less time than that?"

Longarm made a wry face, and said, "Speak for yourself. I hardly ever run a suspect in when I've no idea on Earth what he might be up to. It's your county, so it's your call. But why not wait till we have some answers to the questions I only sent out this very day?"

Wallward replied, "He might make a run for it before you get any answers. Why would he have those riders trailing you if he didn't suspect you were getting warm?"

Longarm laughed bitterly and said, "If I was any colder I'd have to wrap myself in a blanket and build a fire, Walt. The only possible way to connect those other menacing assholes to the menacing placer miner up the creek the other way hinges on the simple fact I haven't the slightest notion what *any* of them could be up to! There's nothing saying the three of them have ever met so far. But I naturally asked the Mounties to see if they had wayward youths called Dakota or Santee on file."

"How did those boys get to be Canadian too?" asked the sheriff.

Longarm said, "We can't even say the man calling himself Tall Tom hails from up yonder yet. Even if we do establish Canada or the Tidewater country further south as his place of birth, it's nowhere writ on stone that the real Plowright family couldn't have moved from most anywhere to Indiana. Down in Dodge I met the Masterson brothers from Canada, the Thompson brothers from England, and a morose dentist called Holliday who said he came from Baltimore. Others said he never did. In any case, we can't write anything off as impossible before we know the real story."

The sheriff frowned and insisted, "But you just said you suspected all three of 'em hailed from Canada, Custis."

Longarm shook his head. "No, I never did. I said the tall one here in Wolverine talks sort of Canadian or Chesapeake. The one they call Dakota didn't, but the Dakota Territory is close to the border, and so is the Santee hunting grounds that other one's named after. I haven't had the chance to talk to him yet."

The older lawman still looked so puzzled Longarm added, "Hell, I'm grasping at straws, Walt. Didn't you just hear me say that spooky is the only thing they have in common for certain? It's an even money bet we're seeing tigers in the roses and there's no connection at all!"

"Tigers in the *what*?" the sheriff demanded.

Longarm replied, "In the roses—say on the wallpaper of a bedroom inhabited by a kid blessed with a vivid imagination and a fear of falling darkness. The artist who designed the wallpaper only meant to show pretty flowers growing all over that bedroom wall. But with nightfall closing in and shadows shifting over on yonder wall, who's to say for certain that ain't a growly tiger crouched among the vines, or an even meaner troll grinning out at you from the wallpaper, just waiting for it to get a tad darker."

Wallward nodded in sudden understanding. "A nightshirt hanging in the wardrobe scared the shit out of me when I was six or seven, now that I think back. You're suggesting we could be making a chess game out of simple tic-tac-toe?"

Longarm rose. "I've done so in the past, Walt. Meanwhile, I'd best tend to my pony, run a razor over my fool face, and see if I can convince the *Wolverine Free Press* you're Montana's answer to Deadwood Dick."

Wallward rose as well, but protested, "There ain't no Deadwood Dick. He's a made-up hero in one of them Wild West magazines."

But Longarm said soothingly, "That's all right. Silas Mullens *reads* Wild West magazines, going by the way he thinks a real sheriff ought to wave his guns around, and I've met two drunks who claim to be the one and original Deadwood Dick so far. I understand there's a heap of colorful cowhands named Richard who've decided that magazine had *them* in mind."

The sheriff followed Longarm back out to his tethered pony. As Longarm untied the reins the older lawman held out a hand. "Go tidy your ownself up and I'll have my own boys rub her down and put her away with plenty of water and cracked corn."

Longarm hesitated, then handed over the reins, saying, "Well, I don't have any dirty pictures in my saddlebags and it's getting a mite late."

So they both went on back and parted friendly by the corral so Longarm could go on up to the guest room, peel off his shirt, and clean up at the corner washstand. Once he'd shaved there as well, he put on the fresh shirt he'd hung to air in the wardrobe the night before. It wasn't really cold enough outside for his denim jacket, but he put it back on anyway, and knotted his silk bandanna under his shirt collar as if it was a real necktie.

He met Flo Wallward out on the stairs as he was fixing to leave. When she said her husband had just told her he'd been invited to sup down the way, he assured her it was strictly business. She told him she'd leave some apple pie and cheese out for him in case he was hungry when he came back.

Then she asked if he'd wired all those theatrical booking agents she'd suggested. So he had to explain what he'd done to her as well. He was starting to worry about the time as he finally strode out front and swung down the walk to head for the Mullens place. But as he consulted his pocket watch in the slanting sunlight, it told him he'd hurried more than he'd really needed. It wasn't five-thirty yet and here he was loping along the walk as if he had another hard-on for old Bathsheba.

He knew she'd figure that if he showed up a whole half hour early. So he ducked inside that Big Belt Saloon, hoping nobody would spot him from the nearby newspaper office. He ignored the cold cuts piled at one end of the bar, and moved down to where the barkeep was jawing with one of the cowhands he'd seen around town before.

When he ordered a schooner of draft the cowhand asked him, in a casual way, if those friends of his had finally caught up with him.

Longarm reached for the beer schooner as casually as he asked who they might be talking about.

The Wolverine rider said, "They never gave their names. I never ask nosy questions when I meet strangers on the trail. But the two of 'em seemed friendly enough. I was coming down the Helena trail off the Slash Bar Seven when I met them going the other way at a trot. I reined out of their way and they stopped to ask if by any chance I'd seen that deputy from Denver, as they'd heard you were on your way to Helena and they had a message for you."

Longarm sipped at his beer to give himself time to think before he replied, "They never caught up with me. Might one of 'em been dressed in black, with his pal wearing a dove-gray hat and a buckskin shirt?"

The plainer-dressed working hand nodded brightly and said, "Yep. That's them to a T. Only the other one's shirt was more army dress blue than black."

"Which way did they go afterwards?" Longarm asked.

The cowhand shrugged and replied, "I wasn't watching. They never rode back with me, if that's what you meant. They might have figured I'd missed you and ridden on up to Helena."

"Or doubled back this way," Longarm decided, confiding to his beer suds, "I was in no position to say, having my own riding to do further down the river. I'd best go see if anyone noticed them riding into town earlier."

He paid for the beer he'd barely touched and strode back outside. He retraced his steps to the sheriff's office and went inside to tell Walt Wallward what he'd just heard. But the sheriff wasn't at his desk. A kid deputy Longarm had only nodded to once, but recalled as a Jimmy Something, glanced up from the paper he was reading at the desk to say, "Evening. Just put your pony away if you want to ride on after the boss and Deputy Gilchrist."

When Longarm asked why in thunder he'd want to do that, the kid explained, "Sheriff Wallward's decided to bring in that mysterious Tall Tom on a suspicion charge. He's afraid the rascal will skip town before we get some messages back from up Canada way and . . ."

Longarm was already leaving by the time the boy could finish. The exasperated federal deputy tore around to the back to rope the roan this time. As he was cinching his McClellan on the fresher mount Flo Wallward stuck her head out upstairs to call down, "What are you up to now, Custis? I thought you were having supper at the Mullens place at six!"

He called back, "It ain't six yet, but you know what that poet said about the best-laid plans of mice and men, Miss Flo. Do you know how far up the creek that placer claim of the so-called Tall Tom might lay?"

She said she for land's sake had no idea. Longarm thanked her anyway, mounted up, and tore out to the street to swing downstream first, in an attempt to repair some social damage.

Bathsheba Mullens came out on the side porch to assure him she understood, but that her Aunt Sadie had invited two aldermen and their wives to supper as well and seemed hardly likely to ever forgive him. When the auburn-haired beauty asked why he couldn't just have supper with them and leave early, he said he'd try to get back in time for dessert. She said she'd save something sweet for him. It would have been taking a chance to kiss her there, with the sun still shining, so he didn't.

He'd meant what he'd said about trying to get right back. So he loped the roan the length of town and beyond as the sun sank ever lower behind them. Fortunately, he didn't have far to lope before he spotted old Walt, that spooky giant, and the younger lawman that had to be Gilchrist jawing between the trail and the creek beside a long rambling sluice cobbled together from raw lumber of various sizes and variety. As Longarm reined in and dismounted near the ponies the two lawmen had tethered to some aspen, the sheriff called out, "Thought you were having supper down the other way.

97

Come and study on this half-ass placer operation and tell me if you've ever seen a Chinaman build such a useless sluice."

Longarm ambled over as the mysterious so-called placer miner was protesting, "It's a free country, damn it. You sluice-placer *your* way and let me worry about how I do *mine!*"

Longarm glanced down at the absolutely pointless box-like length of so-called sluice. He laughed and said, "Correct me if I'm wrong, but the way this Chinaman explained it to me, you shovel sand in one end and running water carries it down a long shallow incline over a lot of cross-board ripples and mayhaps a few yards of plush carpet material. The thesis is that heavier grains of placer gold ought to settle in the ripples if they're around the same size as the far lighter sand grains. You have to burn the carpet material now and again to sift the ash for really fine grains."

Deputy Gilchrist snorted, "That would be if there was one grain of even fool's gold in this thoroughly prospected creek!"

Wallward nodded and demanded, "How about that, stranger? I know you filed a lawful claim on all this sand and gravel, but 'fess up and tell us if you've ever found a flea's fart of color here!"

The tall mysterious stranger shrugged and muttered, "I'm still working on my sluice, as anyone but a total idjet ought to be able to see for hisself. These things take time, you know, and it hasn't been easy, shopping for nails and such, with you gents mean-mouthing me in town."

"I'll mean-mouth you in town," the sheriff declared, turning to Gilchrist to add, "Cuff the cuss and let's carry him back to spend a while on the county, Dan."

Gilchrist looked uncertain as he asked, "What's the charge, in case some lawyer asks, Sheriff?"

Wallward said, "Suspicion, of course."

The taller suspect protested, "Hold on. Suspicion of what?"

So the sheriff spat, "Suspicion of acting suspicious, you suspicious rascal! Who gave you call to traipse around using a dead man's name whilst claiming bare-ass sand as a gold placer?"

"Name me one law I've broken," the sinister giant demanded in a defiant tone.

Wallward dropped a hand to the grips of his six-gun, but Longarm warned, "Don't, Walt! He's got you on statute law in front of witnesses. George Sand, Mark Twain, and a heap of others would be in deep shit if it was against the law to change your name just for the hell of it. The courts hold it's only unlawful to give a false name when it can be proven you did so to flimflam somebody out of something. What were you fixing to tell this jasper's lawyer he was obtaining under false pretenses, Walt?"

The older man swore like a safety valve about to pop, and pointed at the nearby contraption of mismatched planking as he insisted, "If that ain't a swindle of some kind it sure as shit ain't no gold sluice!"

"*I* like it," said its owner smugly.

Before the sheriff could pistol-whip him Longarm said, "It's his right under federal mining law, Walt. If it was unlawful to prospect stupid, the prisons would be overflowing with failed prospectors. Ninety-nine out of a hundred gold rushers never pan two bits worth of color. But nobody puts them in jail for trying."

Wallward almost sobbed, "Custis, this cuss ain't trying! That pointless waste of firewood wouldn't work as a gold sluice if there was a high-grade placer in that creek!"

The sardonic stranger calling himself Thomas Plowright purred so smugly Longarm wanted to hit him too as he

99

asked mildly, "Then what's all the fuss about, Sheriff? Your deputy here just told us there's no color at all in Wolverine Creek."

Wallward said, "That does it. You're under arrest, you smug-ass son of a bitch!"

Longarm would have tried to talk them out of it. But just then the ground tingled under them as the sunset sky to the west was rent by a tremendous blast.

As the echoes still rumbled up and down the valley the sheriff declared, "That was no dry lightning! That was dynamite, a heap of dynamite, and it sounded like it just went off in town!"

Longarm was already moving for his tethered pony. Behind him the sheriff was declaring, "Let's go, Dan. You too, Tall Tom or whoever the hell you really are. We'll talk about booking you after we find out what that was we heard just now!"

Longarm was already mounted and moving out, afraid he knew. The explosion hadn't been muffled enough for a stump blast or a safe blowing, and nobody used that much dynamite at once unless they wanted to blow the shit out of something as big as a house.

It was along about six-thirty and he was riding fast for town when Lester Kenmore and couple of his vigilantes came tear-assing the other way, waving their guns as Kenmore demanded, "See any others riding the other direction up this way?"

Longarm reined in just long enough to reply, "Not a soul. What's up in town, Kenmore?"

The hard-eyed stockman cum vigilante called back, "Not up. *Down!* Some sons of bitches just threw a bomb through Silas Mullens' window to level the place and kill every living soul inside as they'd just set down to supper!"

Chapter 8

It took time and considerable torchlight to gather enough body parts for an inquest in the tilted but still-standing office of the *Wolverine Free Press*. Nobody else wanted to clean up afterwards, and the big flatbed press that now seemed free for the taking had stopped a heap of shattered debris from the quarters out back.

You could still see Bathsheba Mullens had been pretty, even with her clothes, half her face, and one fondly remembered tit torn away. They figured she'd be furthest from the dynamite bomb some son of a bitch had hurled through the window over her uncle's shoulder. It was sort of tough to say which ripped-off limbs went with which torso, but they were pretty sure they had all the heads right. You could tell a lot from hair, teeth, and such, even after a head had been blown through lath and plaster like a soggy cannon ball.

Longarm had been busy pestering shopkeepers at home as the full-time horse doctor and part-time coroner got things sort of sorted out in the wrecked newspaper press room. So he didn't have to sit through a lot of wild speculation before he came in, crunching busted glass, to tell the others around the mangled remains on the floor, "Nobody here in

Wolverine sold dynamite to anyone in recent memory. Mister Greenberg, as runs the only hardware selling explosives, tells me he sells mostly black powder for stump blasting and other such agricultural chores. Dynamite's not only more costly, but better for shattering hardrock than pushing up stumps or blowing postholes in hard pan."

When another old-timer said everyone knew there was no hardrock mining around Wolverine, Longarm replied mildly, "I just said that. Mister Greenberg says he ordered some forty-percent DuPont for the old boys who sank that coyote shaft to bedrock two or three years ago. He says they left town when they never hit anything but granite, and I agree that blast we all heard sounded more like sixty-percent intended for a serious shattering."

The coroner grimaced down at the mangled bodies at their feet as he muttered, "They surely shattered these poor souls. Seven people, blown to Kingdom Come just as they were having their first course!"

Longarm said, "Eight might have been the intended score. For I'd have been sitting there with 'em if I hadn't been called away at the last moment. I've been studying on just who in town might have known I'd been invited to supper out back this evening. The trouble is, almost anyone in town could have known, once Miss Sadie invited two aldermen and their wives to join us there. I understand she was a punctual lady too, known for always serving the first course at six on the nose."

Walt Wallward offered, "Just like my Flo. All the respectable women in Wolverine serve supper at the same time, Custis."

Longarm sighed and muttered, "I just said that. Anyone asking for me around town could have heard, innocently, I was expected at six for supper with these poor folks. I already heard two strangers were in town asking about me earlier.

102

They could have brought all the dynamite they needed from the more serious gold fields up Helena way."

He reached absently for a cheroot, decided this was neither the time nor place, and continued. "I could be bragging too. Old Silas Mullens, if that's him there, had plenty of enemies of his own, and Lord only knows who'd be after a town alderman in an election year."

A cowhand who'd ridden with Lester Kenmore shook his head and said, "We never had much in the way of killings until recent. I vote we go have us a talk with that stranger calling his fool self by a dead outlaw's name as he sluices pure sand for no good reason the rest of us can see!"

Walt Wallward grinned at Longarm in the grim lamplight as he told the vigilante, "You can't, Clay. The suspect's locked up in my county jail even as we speak. You self-appointed lawmen ain't the only ones with any imagination, you know. We got that old boy locked away in durance vile till he commences to make more sense or till Longarm here finds out who in blue blazes he's really been all this time!"

Longarm shot the sheriff a dirty look as he saw he was expected to explain to the coroner's whole damned jury. Once he'd done so, in as few terse words as possible, the old horse doctor decided, "In that case I mean to adjourn this hearing till Longarm can get back from that Western Union in Helena with more answers. Anyone can see the immediate cause of these deaths was dynamite. So we'll just box 'em and bury them and worry about who dynamited 'em after we get us a more sensible list of suspects. Neither Dakota nor Santee add up to proper names, and nobody but Longarm here knows what they look like!"

Longarm let it go at that. He saved himself some breath, if not a heap of time, by not pointing out those strange riders had asked any number of others around town about him. For by this late in the game it seemed just as obvious the sons of bitches were long gone. Nobody in the small community remembered seeing any strangers riding in or out after that horrendous dynamite blast had brought everyone out of doors in the last good light of the dying day.

The sheriff nudged Longarm and suggested they go back to his place and let Flo make up for his having missed his supper. But Longarm was still feeling sick to his stomach and said so, adding, "I can eat in Helena later if the long ride ever kills the green taste for me. I *liked* those folks on the floor, Walt."

The sheriff said, "Well, you'll want an early start come morning, and I'll still bet you're hungry as a bitch wolf long before you can make it that far, old son."

Longarm said he was wound too tight to even think about bedding down this side of midnight. He added, "I can make Helena not much later if I start right now. Could I borrow a couple of fresher ponies from your remuda, though?"

The sheriff said sure, and the two of them legged it on up the street to the lockup. When Wallward asked if Longarm wanted to ask their tall suspect any more questions, Longarm made a wry face and said, "I wish you wouldn't include me in that arrest. By rights you ought to have a town constable and let Justice Steiner book pests on misdemeanors such as acting vaguely menacing. It ain't dignified to throw a man in the county jail on such piss-ant charges, Walt."

The sheriff said, "I know. But every time I mention that to the township's board of aldermen, the cheap bastards tell me they don't need no town marshal with me set up as the county law right here in town."

Longarm considered that, then mused aloud, "I wish you'd quit offering me political angles I hadn't considered before, Walt. Lord knows I have enough to figure out around here as it is!"

As they moved around to the back in the falling darkness, the older man asked if Longarm figured someone out to make him look bad as the combined town and county law had blown up all those poor souls while he was away with some such mean-mouthing in mind.

Longarm said he didn't see how that would work, pointing out such a malicious gossip would have to tip his hand in the bombing just by shooting his mouth off. He said, "Someone's gone to a whole lot of trouble if all they meant in the end was to call you a poor lawman. Poor old Silas Mullens was doing that for them already."

The sheriff gasped, "Jesus H. Christ! Ain't lots of folk likely to think somebody on *my* side throwed that bomb through the window of a political enemy?"

Longarm said, "I already considered that. Aside from the perfect alibi I can offer you personally, I was on your side and the killer or killers knew it when they hurled that dynamite. Couldn't have been half a dozen in town who knew I wasn't at table with the rest of 'em, and none of the rest of you work worth spit as suspects. You know your own riding stock better than me, Walt."

The sheriff said, "I got a good red bay and a paint you might like. As I follow your drift, hardly anybody that didn't get blown up had any way of knowing you weren't in there with 'em, right?"

Longarm nodded. "Even better, anyone in cahoots with the bomb thrower would have called the attack off after they'd seen I wasn't supping with the *Wolverine Free Press* after all. But like the coroner said, let's quit running in circles like a pup chasing its own tail till we get some answers. Come this time tomorrow, we'll know better whether that cuss in your lockup is named Thomas Plowright or something else entire."

The sheriff asked, "How are we going to prove he heaved

all that dynamite no matter who the hell he might be?"

Longarm sighed. "We can't. Next to you, me, and your Deputy Gilchrist, he's got a tighter alibi than anyone else in town!"

Longarm got back to Helena after midnight. The long ride in the clean cool mountain air had conspired with the rage replacing his first numb shock to remind him he hadn't eaten in a hell of a spell.

There wasn't much open that late on a weeknight in a town where most men had to be at work at sunrise this time of the year. Some of the oil-fired street lamps had already flickered out as Longarm and his two ponies clip-clopped along the nearly deserted main street into town from the river crossing. He recalled one all-night beanery near the main livery and town corral, but first things coming first and his ponies having served him well, he rode into the livery yard to demand some damned service.

A gimpy old colored hostler he'd dealt with in the past limped out into the tricky light of a nearby street lamp as Longarm dismounted. Since they knew one another, Longarm didn't threaten the older man with bodily harm if he fed the ponies before they'd been watered good and given a breathing spell. There was no point in insulting an old pro by directing him to secure his saddle in their tack room and rub down both his pals down before putting them away for the night. But as the hostler took the reins Longarm said, "I'll bet you two bits extra you wouldn't recall two recent arrivals on bay ponies, one wearing black pants and an old dress-cavalry shirt, with his pal wearing buckskin and a dove-gray Stetson?"

The old-timer sighed and said he couldn't help the cap'n. Longarm handed him the quarter anyway, and said, "There's more where that came from if you'd care to join me in a little skullduggery."

The older and likely world-weary colored hand allowed he could go along with anything that didn't involve getting him in bad with other white lawmen. So Longarm explained, "The odds are better than even that nothing at all is going to transpire at this hour. On the other hand, this *is* where I turned in to board my ponies after such a long ride, and you know what they say about great minds running in the same channels."

"You expects them gents you be looking for to turn in here, Cap'n?" the hostler asked with an uncertain grin.

Longarm nodded. "Fifty-fifty. They may have left Wolverine Township well ahead of me. On the other hand I was riding direct, without cutting back and forth to throw trackers off my trail. Suffice it to say, I mean to sort of hang around a spell to watch from the shadows across the way. Do I really have to tell you what I'd like you to say if anyone else rides in to ask if you've seen hide or hair of me this evening?"

The old hostler's grin grew more certain as he innocently asked who they could be talking about, business being so slow all evening.

Longarm gave him another two bits and they parted friendly.

As the hostler led the two ponies out of sight, Longarm ambled off to admire a notions shop across the way. It was closed and shuttered for the night. So you couldn't stare through the glass at all the ribbon bows and yard goods they sold by daylight. You couldn't even see the shutters from any distance, as dark as the shadows of the overhead awning fell across the plank walk. So Longarm lit a smoke, stepped up on the planks, and turned to hunker down with his back to the shop's locked door, shielding the ruby tip of his cheroot in his cupped left hand.

He naturally had his gun hand on the grips of the .44–40 resting in his lap. Quick-draw contests were for characters in

Ned Buntline's Western Library, or a real-life lawman who ran into unexpected trouble. At the moment Longarm knew he could expect either a serious discussion at two-to-one odds, or a long tedious wait for nothing at all.

He smoked the first cheroot away to a mustache-endangering stub, and tried not to light another as a million years went by and another street lamp guttered out down the way. Then, just after he'd lit his second smoke, he heard hoofbeats and cupped it tight. The ice ages came and went. Rome rose and fell. Then he could make out the lone rider walking his bay in across the way. The hat was wrong, but the shirt was tan flannel or buckskin. Longarm sat tight as the dimly lit rider dismounted and jawed a spell with the old colored man on the far side of the mighty dim-lit street. Then the hostler had the stranger's pony by the reins, and the murky cuss was walking off on foot up the wrong damned side of the street.

Longarm slid up the door to glide the same way in his low-heeled army boots, hugging the shadows and staying off his heels. He wore the sometimes awkward footgear for riding because a lawman spent a mite more time on his feet than your average cowhand, and because there were times, such as this, when clanging spurs or clunking heels could mess up a stalk entirely. On the far side of the street his man was clunking and clanging as if to wake the dead.

Longarm waited till they came to a really dark patch of piss-poor street lighting, and let the other man get a tad ahead before he lightly moved across the way on the balls of his own feet.

The other man still detected movement behind him, and spun to drop a thoughtful hand to the grips of his side-draw six-gun. Then Longarm threw down on him to warn, not unkindly, "Let go your side arm and grab some sky if you'd like to see sunrise, Dakota."

The foolishly shirted kid reached high indeed as he let out a startled gasp and called back, "I give! I give! I know what you're thinking but I wasn't with him, Longarm! I told Santee this child was only good for running folks off, not for sticking his poor neck in no noose! I left as soon as they started talking about dynamite and not caring if fool womenfolk got in the way!"

Longarm moved closer, saying, "Keep it down. We don't want all the neighbors coming out to join this private conversation, Dakota. They dynamited four women all told. Now you're fixing to tell where I can find Santee and who the they were you mentioned in the plural tense just now."

Dakota sort of pleaded, "I don't know where Santee went after we split up back near Wolverine. I don't know the name of that older cuss who hired us. Santee was the one who did most of the talking for the both of us. But I heard him tell Santee he'd had enough fooling around with you and wanted you dead. When Santee pointed out neither of us were about to take on a gunslick of your rep in even a two-on-one, he said he knew where you'd been invited to supper and that he'd been saving up some dynamite with just such an emergency in mind."

Longarm nodded grimly and said, "It was sixty-percent DuPont, the son of a bitch. What did he look like, if you don't know his name?"

Dakota licked his lips and said, "Maybe I could give you his name, if we could have us some firm understandings about the way things turned out back yonder."

Longarm raised a dubious eyebrow. "Keep talking. I can deal as well as the next lawman, to a point. I reckon you know the point of no return, don't you?"

Dakota insisted, "I ain't asking you to let me off on no killing! I swear I never killed nobody. I swear I crawfished out of the deal as soon as I heard them say shit about really killing anybody!"

Longarm hesitated, then said, "All right. I can say I'd have no call to arrest an old boy on a murder charge after he was the one who told me who the killers were."

Dakota insisted, "I want your word I don't even have to appear anywhere as a witness. I tell you who and I tell you where I last saw Santee and we just turn and walk away from here in opposite ways, agreed?"

Longarm said, "With one proviso. All bets are off if you lie or hold back one fucking fact. What's Santee's real name and who were the two of you working for? Right now, with no more shilly-shally."

Dakota said, "Santee's real name is Gaston Dupres and he's from Canada. We teamed up in the Dakota Territory, and I ain't sure just where and when Santee met up with that Lester cuss as heads the vigilance committee around Wolverine."

"Lester Kenmore was the one who ordered Silas Mullens and all the rest of us blown up like that?" gasped Longarm in genuine surprise.

Dakota kept his hands up as he shrugged and said, "I suspect it was you they had in mind as the main target, Longarm. That Lester cuss never said why he was so sore at you, but he never called you sweetheart when he said he wanted us to make sure of you after we blew you up."

Longarm decided, "I'll ask old Lester about that. I need a better description of your pal Santee. For all I've heard about the sinister cuss, I've yet to lay eyes on him up close."

Dakota said, "He ain't one to stand out in no crowd. But I reckon you could pick him out by his chin hair and stature. He don't shave when he's hired out his gun hand. Lets his beard grow in hopes he'll be remembered that way when he picks up his pay, changes his duds, and shaves."

Longarm asked, "What was that about his stature?"

Dakota said, "Oh, he's a little runty cuss. Used to be a jockey, he says." Then Longarm dropped to the plank walk and rolled off to hit the dusty street on his gut and fire back as a six-gun blazed in the darkness his fool back had been facing all this time.

He whirled to cover Dakota as he heard the sneaky rascal wailing, "Not me, you asshole, *him*!" But he didn't fire as the buckskin-clad bullshit artist collapsed like a punctured bladder to sprawl in a shapeless heap. Then Longarm pegged another round into the darkness for luck, rose, and dashed for the better cover of a doorway broadside to the direction of those running footsteps.

Longarm started after them, but stopped when they did. For any man who'd charge blind into darkness after another he didn't know on sight was a man who'd never been in a serious gunfight before!

As windows and doors up and down the street popped open and the town started waking and lighting up, Longarm got out his federal badge and pinned it to the front of his denim jacket as he strode over to the fallen Dakota gun in hand. He hunkered down to removed the kid's own side arm from its holster as he said conversationally, "I said I'd never laid eyes on your pal up close. I never said not ever. I watched the two of you riding off from across a river one time. I may not have the eyes of an eagle, but I could see you were both clean-shaven and about the same size. Why didn't you just describe him accurately as he was getting set up behind me? You were slick enough to ride in separate, with him covering for you whilst you saw whether I was in town or not."

Dakota didn't answer. Longarm struck a match and held it over the kid's blankly staring eyes. He nodded, shook it out, and said, "I was wondering why Lester Kenmore would want to murder a newspaper man who kept praising him and his vigilantes. Made no sense for him to kill a pretty gal he'd just tried to save from kidnapping rapists as well."

He heard boot heels coming his way in a mighty authoritative manner, and rose to look as authoritative with his own badge shining better in the poor light.

Then he nudged the dead liar with a thoughtful boot tip and said aloud, "On the other hand, a jealous swain who suspected his true love had been messing with an outsider could get sore enough to bomb most anybody. Damn it, Dakota, I sure wish I knew how much truth and falsehood you might have been mixing as you stalled for time just now!"

Chapter 9

Within the hour Longarm had explained the situation thrice to four times that many local lawmen. The third time was tedious, but repeating yourself was a good way to organize your thinking. When old Clinkers, the Helena lawman he'd talked to before, asked him whether he thought Santee had shot Dakota by mistake or to shut him up, Longarm said, "It works either way, and we don't know for certain it was his pal Santee. He said they'd both been working for somebody else he described as a remorseless killer."

They were talking out front of the Helena morgue, where Clinkers had caught up with Longarm and the night shift after hearing about the shooting at home. The chill night air reminded Longarm how long it had been since he'd last eaten, and inspired him to look for some place a tad warmer in his thin denim jacket. But first things had to come first, so he told Clinkers, "You've seen this Santee jasper in the flesh. So you're one up on me. But I take it he wasn't really a bearded midget when he came to tell you Dakota was starting up with yours truly that time?"

Clinkers said, "Not hardly. I'd describe Santee as a few years older but about the same height and build as Dakota.

Has light hair and gray eyes, I think. Wears plainer duds than Dakota did, but you would never mistake him for anything but a cowboy, unless it was a road agent. High heels, big ringing spurs, and a low-slung *buscadero* gunbelt with fancy tooling and German silver fittings."

Longarm asked if Santee looked or talked like a Metis, or wilder breed of French Canadian.

Clinker said, "Didn't know he was any sort of French Canadian. Looked and talked like a regular old boy to me. Maybe not quite as twangy as a rider from south of the Platte or Cumberland watersheds. Talked more like Jim Hickok used to, before he got back-shot over in Deadwood that time."

Longarm nodded. "Illinois, I think he said he came from. Learned to shoot as a market hunter along the shores of the Great Lakes. That used to be Santee country too. Dakota was likely just shitting me when he said his pal was Canadian. Might not be any Canadians involved at all. Meanwhile I'm hungry enough to eat my hat, and a few hours sleep wouldn't kill me either."

Clinkers and the night watch commander agreed Longarm's signed statement ought to hold the local coroner's jury, seeing he'd only witnessed the demise of Dakota and likely hadn't hit anybody his own self. So they shook on it and parted friendly.

The tired and hungry Longarm found an all-night beanery catering to night owls around the Overland Stage Depot, and ate enough pork and beans with fried potatoes to knock him half off his feet. So he explained how awful he felt to the Overland manager, and they hired him a room upstairs, even though he didn't want to board the coach to Virginia City in the cold gray dawn.

He slept damned nearer to noon, behind a locked door nobody but a handful of total strangers had ever seen him open. Hence he left the stage depot bright-eyed and bushy-tailed, as well as ashamed of the hours of daylight he'd wasted slugabed. So he ordered chili over a couple of fried eggs, with raisin pie and plenty of black coffee to get his head working before he ambled over to the Western Union.

Once there, he found his Canadian pal, Crown Sergeant Foster, had wired answers to some but not all the questions he'd asked the Mounties to look into for him.

None of the first answers were any help to him. He'd forgotten whether it had been William of Ockham or some other old-time lawman who'd said it meant you were asking the wrong questions when you didn't get sensible answers. But the notion made sense. So Longarm picked up a blank telegram form and licked the lead tip of a stub pencil as he tried to figure what he ought to ask whom next. Then he put things back the way he'd found them and told the telegraph clerk he'd come back later, maybe to send some wires after he'd had time to read some more and study on what he needed to know.

He had to ask directions to the Helena Grange Hall. Once he found it padlocked, he circled around to discover some side steps and, at the top, a smaller door marked "NATIONAL GRANGE OF THE PATRONS OF HUS-BANDRY, MONTANA CHAPTER." He opened the door and went on in.

He found himself in a reception room with a young gal who was sort of pretty, if one admired mice. She was seated behind a big desk in a mouse-gray bodice guarded at the base of her throat by a cameo brooch. Her hair wasn't really gray when you looked twice. It was more the color of the fuzz you find under the beds of an ill-kept boarding house. Her steel-rimmed specs made her gray eyes look even bigger as she stared up at him as if he'd come to rob the place. So he quick-ly produced the federal badge he'd put back out of casual sight as he told her who he was and what he'd come for.

She told him in a little mousy voice to have a seat while she went to see if anyone wanted to talk to him. The only place to sit was a hard bench with the wall behind it stained by the backs of a heap of sweaty shirts. There was a *Farmer's Almanac* on an end table. But Longarm didn't really care how well last year's winter wheat was likely to fare. And he had the edge on the old boys who'd predicted more heat and drought on the High Plains. He'd already lived through a wet spring and a nicer than usual summer.

The mousy gal came back and said her boss would see him if only he would walk her way. He couldn't have walked her way if he'd wanted to, but he followed the surprisingly jiggly little thing back to the bigger but more cluttered office of a professed Granger who looked a lot more like a banker to a man who'd grown up on a real farm.

The well-dressed and manicured son of the soil said his name was Granger Maxwell and they started out friendly enough, with Longarm offered a comfortable seat and a medium-priced cigar. But as soon as Longarm said he'd like to go over that fall's slate of candidates for public office on the Granger ticket, the boss Granger smiled as sincerely as a hen-killing yard dog and said he was not at liberty to give away party secrets.

Longarm said, "Aw, hell, you're going to have to announce in the next few weeks if you expect anyone to vote for any of your mystery candidates. Meanwhile, I'm investigating mass murder, including the murder of Silas Mullens of your very own party."

Maxwell nodded soberly. "We just heard about those Black Republicans putting our *Wolverine Free Press* out of business with an infernal explosion. I'm not about to expose our other friends to danger by giving out their names a day sooner than I really have to!"

Longarm puffed ferociously on the mild cigar and growled, "Hang a wreath on you face. Your brain just died. Can't you see the best way to keep anyone else from getting killed would be to help me catch the damned killers before they can strike again? I ain't no black nothing. I'm a paid-up U.S. deputy marshal, confused as hell but, damn it all, trying to make *sense* of all this shit!"

"While working for a republican administration," Maxwell sniffed in a far from barnyard manner as he fished out a fancy watch to gaze at it in a far from subtle way.

Longarm smiled incredulously and asked, "Do you really suspect the current republican administration of These United States would blow folks up just to have its own way?"

Maxwell shrugged. "Abe Lincoln was a Republican, and ask folks back home in Atlanta how many of us he blew up before he'd had his way!"

Before Longarm could answer Maxwell added, "Tell me your boss, the Honorable Rutherford Hayes, won his *last* election fair and square, if you dare! Everybody knows he stole the presidency from Sam Tilden with the help of a partisan electoral college!"

Longarm nodded. "You just made my point, sir. I'll go along with Sam Tilden mayhaps really getting a few more popular votes. I'll even go along with partisan deals in smoke-filled rooms, if only you would allow that the major parties seldom resort to anything clumsy as mass murder. For openers, they don't have to. I'm betting on somebody who can't promise new roads, schools, and such. I'm betting on just a single son of a bitch, out to put no more than one or two pals in a local position come November. I don't need to know who the Grange is running all over Montana Territory. Just tell me who your candidate for sheriff might be over in Wolverine. Is that too much to ask?"

Granger Maxwell said it was, adding, "It's not up to me alone. I have to answer to others, and they'd have my hide nailed to the wall if I gave away party secrets to outsiders!"

Longarm said he'd heard the Knights of Labor were a secretive bunch too as he rose to leave, though not before he pointed out it would be on Maxwell's head if anyone else got blown to Kingdom Come.

On his way back to the Western Union he passed the vaudeville theater, where an elderly gent was posting three-sheets informing the public that the Four Cohans and Cycling McNutts, among others, would soon be astounding Montana Territory with their wondrous acts, direct from their triumphs in Paris, London, and Louisville.

Longarm ambled over, watched in admiration for a spell, and when the old theater manager asked what he wanted, told him.

The showman proved friendlier than Granger Maxwell, once he saw Longarm didn't want to sell him anything. He said he'd be proud to let a lawman look at his directory of theatrical booking agents as soon as he was done out front.

It didn't take much longer. Longarm followed the older man into the dank depths of a deserted theater, and they wound up in a bitty office with a rolltop desk. The theater manager told Longarm to take the one seat at the desk as he rummaged in a file cabinet to produce a well-thumbed manila folder with some clipped-together pulp-paper pages in it. He placed them before Longarm on the narrow work space of his cluttered desk as Longarm got his own notebook out.

He blinked in dismay, though, when he saw how many listings even an out-of-the-way theater had to choose from. When he said he'd had no idea so many folks found work for performers, the man in the business chuckled and said, "Some people will do anything for ten percent. A lot of them

118

raise chickens and book dog acts as a sideline."

Longarm said, "I'm more worried about a possible actor doing odd jobs for Lord knows how much. I reckon I can eliminate every agency east of, say, Chicago. It would still be a big help if you could say yes or no as I check off some names out loud."

It helped indeed. The better-versed showman was able to assure him more than half the Western listings were pissants he'd never really dealt with. That still left him with far more listings than old Flo Wallward had suggested. When he showed her list to the theater manager, he was told she'd left out a handful of smaller agencies that might still do business with the sort of squirts who did trick riding, roping, or shooting for traveling shows. When he said nobody old Flo had left out was likely to book stage shows, Longarm wrote the names down anyway, saying, "The cuss I have in mind could be a Wild West showman. Acts more like a cowman than a stage actor."

That naturally inspired the theater manager to ask more about the case they were working on, and since he'd been so helpful, Longarm felt obliged to tell him the whole story. It took a spell, but you never knew where bread cast on the water was likely to end up. The old-timer said, "I do recall a tall drink of water with a lantern jaw and a scar over one eye, now that I think back over many a bill. He wasn't a trick rider or roper, though. Not if we're talking about the same vaudeville trouper. Damn. I wish I could recall his name. He had a magic act, not a very good one, if the truth be known. But between his appearance and the pretty little gal he sawed in half and stuffed in a basket to be stabbed by swords . . ."

"Stage magic is just what I had in mind!" Longarm declared. "This circus gal I used to know explained that misdirection shit a magician uses to flimflam the rest of us

119

poor souls. I've caught a heap of flimflammers since, using her helpful hints about watching the other hand, not the one moving the shells. All sorts of crooks and confidence men use similar tricks to misdirect the attention of the law. You say this tall scar-faced magician worked with a pretty gal?"

The older man nodded. "Orpheum Circuit, bigger towns to the east, that's where I saw the act, and Lord have mercy, it must have been some time ago indeed. How old did you say this Tall Tom Plowright's supposed to be?"

"Middle-aged, the same as the real Tall Tom. I reckon he could have his hair dyed, if we're talking really old or some other hair color to begin with. I caught a crook a spell back who dyed his blond hair red to fool folks. Ain't that a bitch?"

The theater manager said, "I've been out this way around ten years. Say he was in his thirties or forties, maybe fifteen years ago when I was managing a house on the Orpheum Circuit, he'd be . . ."

"Close enough," Longarm said. "He keeps saying he's a cuss who'd have been in his thirties seven years ago, when I saw him get killed. Most of us keep getting older-looking till we're in our forties. Then we stop and don't look much different, give or take some hair dye, till we're really old."

The old showman sighed and said he'd noticed that, murmuring, "Where are the snows of yesteryear and ain't it a shame how fat they get right after the honeymoon? I wish I could remember *either* of the names that trouper and his gal used long ago and far away. Maybe it'll come to me in the middle of the night."

Longarm said that was when *he* usually recalled such things, and said he might drop by later just in case. Then he returned to the Western Union to follow up on the few new leads by wire. While he was there they gave him some fresh wires from Fort MacLeod. Nobody up Canada way seemed to be looking for a tall lantern-jawed moose with a scar over his infernal left eyebrow.

By this time the whole afternoon had been shot to no avail worth mention. So he went and had some needled beer with boiled eggs and pickled pig's feet at a place that put out a fair free lunch.

He neither ate nor drank too much as he kept an eye on the time. Then, when he figured it was about quitting time, he strode back up to the Grange Hall, picked up some extra smokes in the tobacco shop across the way, and loitered under the overhang with a wooden Indian until, sure enough, that mousy little secretary came down the steps under a mousy straw boater—unescorted, bless her mousy hide.

She almost squeaked, but didn't, when Longarm overtook her around the corner and fell in step beside her with a polite tick of his hat brim. She said, "Oh, it's you. You startled me."

He said, "I never meant to, ma'am. Is there somewhere we could go sit down long enough for me to tell you about another lady who got startled more seriously by the villains I'm trying to track down?"

She looked all about, as if for a way out, then said she lived just down the street and thought it would be respectable enough if they sat out in full view on her porch swing while he had his say.

Longarm said that sounded fair. She naturally wanted to hear all about that other lady long before they got there. But Longarm made her wait, and then *he* had to wait, alone on the side porch of a one-story flat-top frame painted slate blue, as she scurried inside in what seemed a hurry. Gals working in an upstairs office likely had no decent place to shit at work.

But when she came back out she'd replaced her hat with a polka-dot apron and brought along a tin tray piled with

121

coffee and cake. She placed it on the padded seat of the porch swing between them, and said to help himself to some cake as she poured. So he did. It was lemon cheese cake. A mite too sweet. But she made coffee strong and it went just right with her cloying cake if you took it black.

She put cream and sugar in her own, of course, as he told her about the death of Bathsheba Mullens, leaving out some of the gruesome details and deleting all the saucy ones. As he'd hoped she might, the little mouse—whose name, she'd said, was Ellen—thought it was just awful to blow up ladies with dynamite at supper time or any other. When she asked what Longarm wanted her to do about it, he explained, "Your boss, Granger Maxwell, seems to think I'm in league with the Republicans or Democrats, if not the Devil. I'll admit an old pal of mine is running for sheriff a second time, but I swear on my own badge I'm not out to influence a single honest voter this November. I hope to be long gone, case closed, by the time anyone on your own party's slate wins or loses fair and square."

She sipped at her own cup thoughtfully as they both watched the afternoon shadows lengthen a spell. Then mousy little Ellen nodded and said, "You want me to tell you who the Grangers are running for sheriff against the incumbent, Walter Wallward."

It had been a statement rather than a question. Longarm was still cautious as he softly replied, "I can see you're smart enough to see why I need to know, Miss Ellen."

She munched some cake in her mousy way, washed it down, and told him, "I really need the job. This house may not be much, but it's all I have and I have to pay taxes on it after I heat it through the sort of winters we get out this way."

Longarm sighed and said, "Your boss said it would be worth his hide too. Mayhaps I'd feel the same way if I was in your shoes, and hadn't seen Miss Bathsheba Mullens all bloody and dead on a messy printshop floor."

Mousy little Ellen murmured, "I never said I wouldn't. I only said I shouldn't and we're going to have to be awfully careful."

"Don't you know who the Grange is running against Walt Wallward?" Longarm asked.

To which she demurely replied, "Heavens, I don't know who we're putting up for alderman here in Helena, Deputy Long. Granger Maxwell keeps our provisional lists in his office safe, subject to last-minute changes by the party committee."

Then she softly added, "Fortunately, I know the combination. I naturally carry my own key to the front door. The door to the inner office may not have a matching lock, though. I've never tried to get into Granger Maxwell's office when he wasn't there."

Longarm said, "Call me Custis, Miss Ellen, and let me worry about door locks. I got some blades on my old pocket knife that could get a man arrested if he wasn't already the law. How late do you reckon we ought to wait?"

She was grinning like a mean little kid as she decided, "Until it's good and dark, Custis. I don't want anyone to see me walking out with another man, this soon after . . . That's another story."

Longarm said they had time for some stories while they admired the sunset. But she said, "Your ghost story about outlaws coming back from the grave to dynamite people sounds more interesting than anything that's ever happened to little old me. I still think that's who did it. I don't care who he was talking to when the dynamite went off. Would it make any sense for someone backed by the Granger Party to blow up the people putting out the only Granger paper for miles?"

Longarm said, "I might be able to answer that better after you show me who we might be talking about, Miss Ellen. You'd be wearing black if your secret sorrow had transpired recently, right?"

She blazed in a far from mousy way, "So I'm only a grass widow and the worthless brute I married in a moment of lunacy still walks above the graveyard grass. But I'll have you know my papers are final and this property and everything on it is in my name and my name alone!"

"You just said you had to pay taxes on it," he said gently, anxious to change the subject now that he'd discovered she was a divorcée. Some of his best friends were divorcées, but most of them tried to avoid saying such a scandalous word as *divorce*. So he could see why she was wearing sober but regular duds. Most any sort of widow got questioned about their dolorous condition some. Gals who could say their man had fallen down a mine shaft or in front of a train had it easier in a town as small as this one.

They polished off the last of her store-bought cheese cake, and he knew better than to trail in after her when she took that tray in and found her hat again. By this time the sky glowed dull red over the Lewis Range to the west and more than one star had winked on in the purple above the Big Belts to the east. They still sat and swung a spell, since a man who rode with a firm but gentle grip had no call to hurry an edgy little mouse when they had all night. So it was Ellen, in the end, who suggested they'd best go and get it over with before she lost her nerve.

There were few street lamps at that end of town to begin with, and the one out front of the Grange Hall, if anything, made the side wall the stairs went up seem as dark as the pit. Ellen was hardly more than a small shapely shadow as Longarm followed her on up. She unlocked the office door with her own key and they ducked in. There wasn't much light coming in from outside, but she naturally knew her way around the place she worked, and took him by one hand this time to lead him the short way down the hallway behind the reception room to the same office he'd been in that afternoon.

He thumbed a light and lit an oil-fired wall fixture above the boss Granger's now-cleared-off desk. Ellen hunkered down behind it to twirl the tumblers of a waist-high Mosler Brand safe built into a wall of bookcases. When Longarm asked if she had enough light she said, "I think so. I'm already worried about someone seeing that light from outside!"

Then she had the safe open, and straightened up to turn to the desk with three stacked ledgers, saying, "I think the names we'd be proposing down by Wolverine would be in one of these."

It was. But the helpful secretary had just found the entry she was looking for, and said so, when they both heard footsteps on those outside steps. They were coming loud, clear, and sudden.

As Ellen gasped, "Oh, no! We're caught!" Longarm had already blown out the wall fixture and shoved her aside to hunker down and shove the ledgers back in the safe.

He was careful not to slam the massive door as he shut it and spun the dial once for luck on the way back up. Then he had the terrified little gal by the arm and back out in the hall by the time they both heard somebody fooling with that front entrance at the head of those outside stairs.

He whispered, "What's down the other way?"

She whimpered, "More offices. Four, all told, and a broom closet!"

He voted for the broom closet at the far end, hauling her into it without asking her views on the subject as he grasped the inside knob to shut them in. It was crowded as well as pitch dark. He put his left hand and forearm around the front of her to hold her still against him as he hung on to that inside knob with his gun hand. She was so short he'd grabbed the front of her a mite higher than she seemed to think proper. She moved his arm down her bodice hissing, "Do you mind?" as her small but surprisingly firm tits popped over his bony forearm into a doubtless more comfortable position.

There was nothing either of them could do about the way her firm but somewhat larger derriere rode against his upper thighs. He could only hope she'd think that was a pocket full of change shoved into the small of her back like that.

They both sucked in their breaths as, out in the hall, they heard somebody saying, "Damn it, Ralph, I know what I saw from out back just now!"

Ellen didn't have to tell Longarm it was her boss, Granger Maxwell. Then the other cuss said, "See for yourself, Tim. There's nobody back here either. It must have been the moonlight on the glass of your dark office you just saw."

Granger Maxwell said, "Cover me. I'll tell you what I saw with my own eyes when they tell me there's nobody skulking back here in any of the other rooms!"

They heard other doors opening and slamming, along with cussing that made Longarm wish he wasn't in mixed company. Then, as Longarm braced himself, some strong-fisted son of a bitch grabbed the other end of the knob-latch he was hanging on to and gave it a hell of a twist.

Longarm let the knobs turn, but let go of the trembling secretary to brace his left palm against the doorjamb as the cuss outside pulled like an ox team and grunted, "Shit, it's locked. I don't remember locking the damned *brooms* away, though!"

The calmer voice out there suggested, "Maybe your hired gal, Miss Ellen, locked something of her own away for safe-keeping. I'll bet she has all sorts of female shit she'd as soon not have on public display. What do you call them cow udders they use to swish their cunts out with, dutch bags? No shit, Tim, ain't you been getting any from that pretty grass widow?"

Granger Maxwell let go of the other knob, Lord love him, as he laughed and answered, "Surely you jest. That poor little dried-up prune would sandpaper a man's dick raw, if ever he got it *in* her. You know what they say about Mike Callahan leaving her for that Blackfoot squaw in desperation, don't you?"

They were still talking dirty as they drifted off down the hall. Longarm could tell the gal they were talking about was crying in the dark against him. But he didn't let on he'd noticed. He whispered to the flat top of her straw boater, "We'd best let them get well clear of the building before we even step out in the hallway, Miss Ellen. I reckon we've convinced them they were imagining things, but you never can be certain."

She sobbed, louder than he wanted her to, "It's not true! That so-called prospector and full-time drunk never left me for anybody! I threw him out when he got drunk on some of my own money I'd put away for household repairs!"

Longarm murmured, "Keep it down to a roar, Miss Ellen. I noticed you were a house-proud working gal and your private past is no business of the U.S. Justice Department. You'd just found the cuss running on the Granger ticket against my pal, Walt Wallward, this November, remember?"

She muttered murderously, "Nobody married to me ever said anything about dried-out old prunes. We don't *have* anybody running for sheriff against the incumbent down that way."

Longarm scowled in the darkness. "Do tell? How come you'd just said you'd found a name when we had to duck in here so suddenly?"

She explained, "I'd just started reading the entry when I said that. I'd barely finished reading it when we heard the footsteps outside. It said our party members in Wolverine had been trying to get a man called Edward Skane to run for the office on our platform. But they have him listed as undecided and probably out of the race this time. That newspaper man, Silas Mullens, was trying to change his mind."

Longarm thought and decided, "I think I've talked to Ed Skane a time or two casually down Wolverine way. He was on a coroner's jury, not asking much, and I canvassed his general store to see if he sold dynamite. He said he didn't."

She suggested, "A man with dynamite on hand would hardly say so if he'd just used some on somebody, would he?"

Longarm shrugged—she felt it in the confined space—and told her, "We trim 'em to fit the picture by shaving motive from means and opportunity. Most anyone in town that evening had the opportunity, and I agree a gent who runs a general store could get his hands on dynamite if he really wanted some. But after that we're stuck with the motive even a surly storekeeper might have for murdering a fellow party member who'd been trying to get him elected to public office."

She asked, "What if he didn't want to run for public office?"

He said, "Just saying no has dynamite beat. Did that entry mention any qualifications a middle-aged storekeeper has to run for Walt Wallward's badge—aside from his being a Granger, I mean?"

128

Ellen said, "There was something about Mister Skane having been a U.S. marshal one time. Over in the Indian Nation, I think it was."

Longarm thought back, then decided, "Deputy marshal, like me and old Walt maybe. Such lawmen come and go out of Fort Smith, under a fair but firm and sort of crusty federal judge called Isaac Parker. I can check that out easy enough come morning."

She wriggled her smaller self against him impatiently and asked him plaintively, "Can't we leave here earlier than that? I feel certain they've left for good, Custis. Granger Maxwell lives a couple of streets over and it's getting pretty late."

He insisted, "It ain't that late and I've caught many a rabbit by just hunkering down to let 'em circle back. Who was that other cuss with your boss just now?"

She said it had sounded like a less important party man who only worked part time in one of the other offices. Then she reached up to unbutton the top of her bodice, complaining, "It's so stuffy in here. Can you, ah, smell more than my sachet, as close as we seem to be, perforce to keep me from being fired?"

He gallantly assured her the violet and jasmine petals somewhere down yonder under her bodice had only been improved a mite by her warm glow. He could tell she'd washed good under the arms before the fresh bodice had gone on, and that other musky scent from further down was only to be expected from an excited female shut up in the dark with a man she wasn't sore at. He didn't ask if she could smell the way his balls were sweating. They usually could. The female nose was attuned to the body odors of a healthy male the way *his* kind of nose was attuned to *their* alluring stink.

She was breathing sort of funny too as she murmured, "I really need some air, Custis. I'm starting to feel faint, and what would you ever do if I passed out on you in here?"

He replied, "Hold you up, of course. I wouldn't take advantage of your helpless condition, if that's what you're worried about."

She said, "Oh, that's a relief," in a disappointed little voice.

He was sorely tempted to turn her around and kiss her, even though he couldn't have explained how he knew she wanted him to. He didn't do it. There was always the chance he was guessing wrong about a gal who'd yell like hell, and even if he was right, he had enough on his plate without having to worry about gals running to their bosses feeling betrayed by a tumbleweed lover they'd taken a mite too seriously.

So they just cuddled together in the dark, giving off fumes, as they let it get late enough to chance a run for it.

Once they did, they were down the outside steps and off into the night like a pair of giggling kids who'd just pulled off a Halloween prank without getting caught. He said so as he walked her home at a more respectable pace. She agreed it had been fun, and observed the Montana nights doubtless had a lot of secrets most folks would never know anything about.

By then her picket gate was just visible in the moonlight ahead. So he started to slow down, saying, "What your boss don't know can't hurt either of you, and I'll let you know what other secrets I might uncover now that I've at least another fine suspect to consider, Miss Ellen."

She tugged him on, saying, "Those weren't the sort of secrets I had in mind, Custis. There's not a soul watching out front now, and aren't you the least curious about whether I'd sandpaper you raw or not, you shy young thing?"

When he got done laughing Longarm assured her, "That was my gun butt you were teasing with your tailbone, and this may be my only night in your fair city."

As she led him up her garden path she confided, "I'd never be this bold if I thought we had more time, and I wouldn't be bold at all if I thought you'd still be in town long enough to brag about it at the barbershop!"

He assured her he didn't think much of barbershop braggarts either, and once they were inside he agreed they'd attracted enough attention lighting lamps in such a nosy neighborhood.

So he could only tell by the interesting rustles of crisp calico that she seemed to be undressing in what seemed to be the bedroom. By the time he'd found a bedpost to hang his gun and hat on, she was already making the bedsprings creak as she wriggled around down there, pleading with him to hurry and stop teasing her.

He let the rest of his duds land anywhere they had a mind to, and joined her atop the covers, naked as a jay, to haul her small but well-proportioned body in to cure what seemed to be ailing the mousy little thing. But Ellen murmured, with her lips half muffled by his, that she liked it better with her on top. So he rolled on his back and she was all over him, biting his collarbone, rubbing her small but well-packed tits across his bare chest, and grasping his engorged shaft to guide it in as she spread her almost childlike thighs in welcome across his upthrust hips.

Her tiny twat was fortunately slick and wet with the considerable passion of a frustrated full-grown woman. So they managed to fit him in quite nicely. But since great minds seemed to run in the same sly channels, they both laughed as she settled down on him completely stuffed, and he liked her even better, as a pal, when she demurely suggested it might fit better after just a little sanding down.

He could see why she liked to be on top as she moved her womanly but child-sized torso up and down with practiced skill. He tried to hold back, but he couldn't and she felt him coming deep inside her as she went on moving, murmuring, "Thanks for the compliment, but don't you *dare* go soft till I catch up with you!"

He couldn't have gone soft in such surroundings if he'd wanted to, and as she placed a bare heel to the mattress on either side of him to really do some serious bouncing, he certainly didn't want to. He came in her again as she collapsed atop him in a shuddering sobbing blob of pure orgasm that stunned them both to voiceless gasping for a long delighted time. Then Ellen softly purred, "Do you believe I threw my worthless husband out now?"

To which he could only reply, "I surely do, the poor bastard!"

Chapter 10

The mousy grass widow was a perfect hostess until around four in the morning. That was when she woke him up French-style for what he'd hoped was a quick one before breakfast in bed. But the hard-up house-proud resident of a modest-sized metropolis seemed a heap more worried about her neighbors than his breakfast. So after she'd had her wicked way with him again dog-style, Longarm found himself out on the street in the pre-dawn cold, feeling used and abused in one way but just as glad in another.

By the time he'd finished waking up over ham and eggs, griddle cakes, and extra coffee, he was ready to get back to work. So he got back to the Western Union, still walking a mite funny, to find the all-night clerk had taken down a few night letters in answer to the questions he'd sent out at day rates earlier.

No one he could think of had managed to prove anything he could use to arrest anybody. He sent some more wires, more to kill time than because he felt any smarter.

He started to wire Fort Smith. Then he had a better notion, and killed more time reading the *Police Gazette* in a hotel lobby till the town woke up all the way.

At the Helena Federal Building they told him their marshal wasn't back yet. He confided to the clerk he'd spoken to before, "I don't care. What I'd really like to know about is a storekeeper over in Wolverine who says he used to be a deputy marshal out of Fort Smith."

Henry's opposite number asked innocently, "You mean old Ed Skane? He quit the Justice Department years ago. Said some of his Cherokee friends were getting screwed beyond endurance by the government and so he didn't want to work for it no more."

Longarm asked how they knew so much about affairs in the Indian Nation up here in Montana Territory.

The clerk said, "We don't. Ed Skane drinks with some of the boys whenever he's in town. Says he ain't sore at his old pals. It's the crooks in Washington he can't abide. We've been trying to get him to change his mind. We could use a part-timer that far down the river, and it ain't like Grant's Indian Ring is still abusing the Civilized Tribes. Men who rode with Skane say he was a pretty good lawman in his time."

Longarm thought back and said, "I noticed he seemed a strong and silent type of cuss. A lot of the real ones seem modest, and you say paid-up Montana riders know for a fact he was really a U.S. deputy down in the Indian Nation?"

The clerk allowed he'd just said that, and asked what all the fuss was about. So Longarm explained, "I just learned the Grangers wanted Ed Skane to run for sheriff against that Walt Wallward we jawed about before. They say Skane ain't made up his mind but seems reluctant."

The clerk said, "I ain't surprised. Aside from not being young as he once was, Ed's got a thriving general store to run and a family to think of before he goes tearing after owlhoot riders in a sort of unsettled part of this country. What's the matter with the old sheriff they got down yonder?

134

Wallward's been sheriff a good four years and ain't been caught robbing the till yet, has he?"

Longarm got out two cheroots as he thoughtfully answered, "I'd say it boils down to party politics, with the Grangers out to unseat an established old-timer with a candidate about as qualified but not any better. Does Ed Skane have a rep for serious arrests or famous gunplay back when he was packing a federal badge?"

The clerk thought as he accepted a cheroot and let Longarm light it for him. Then he took a drag, let it out, and said, "Hard to tell. We've agreed old Ed ain't one for bragging. The Indian Nation ain't no girls' finishing school. But don't Walt Wallward have a pretty good rep as a one-time federal man hisself?"

Longarm lit his own smoke, shook out the match, and said, "Yep. Like I said, equal choice save for which party you favor. I might feel less confounded if one or the other could be proven a schoolmarm with delusions of grandeur."

The clerk hesitated, then cautiously asked, "Have you considered the mean things Silas Mullens was printing in his Granger paper just before someone blew him up?"

Longarm nodded. "I have. Walt Wallward couldn't have done it personally, but he could have had a henchman lob that bomb if it made more sense for Walt to want *me* dead. I'd just told him I'd been invited to supper there. It ain't that we were in love. It's just that folks generally have a *motive* when they set out to kill me or anybody else."

The clerk asked, "Weren't a lot of other innocent supper guests blown up along with old Silas Mullens?"

Longarm nodded but insisted, "I ain't sure who the bomber was after. Walt sent for me to help him refute some of the mean things Mullens was saying about him in print. That seems a heap of trouble to go to when you're willing and able to murder a newspaper man to shut him up.

On top of that, I'd about convinced old Silas he ought to retract some of the wilder charges against a political opponent, and Walt knew that as well. I know it don't sound modest, but how do you like the notion of me being the main target and Silas and the others being the slaughtered innocents?" –

The clerk agreed he liked that better than any of those victims could have. Then he said, "Don't that put you right back where you started, with nobody having a logical motive for toad squat?"

Longarm swore softly. "It does. The bomber had to know he, she, or it was sacrificing a friend or at least a partisan to get the intended target. So wouldn't that mean either Mullens or me had somebody or other worried as hell about something."

The clerk, who'd doubtless filed a heap of case reports, said, "No. It would mean *somebody killed* had the killer mighty sore or mighty worried about something."

Longarm started to object, then grinned sheepishly and told the clerk, "I needed that. It's all too easy to think the sun came up just because you were the one going cockle-doodle-doo. Two other victims were local politicos. Granger Movement, I'm pretty sure."

Then he swore louder. "Jesus H. Christ, that is a whole new kettle of fish! That bomb could have been lobbed on orders from most anyone to kill any one of seven victims. There has to be a better way."

The clerk asked, with interest, where Longarm meant to start in his search for an easier solution.

Longarm answered, "I only *said* there had to be a better way. I never said I *knew* one. As of now, all I can do is head back the damn way I just came and start asking the same dumb questions of the same dumb folks in the same dumb town."

The clerk pointed out the dumb fact that at least one person in Wolverine knew some answers. Longarm allowed he'd just said that, and left to do some riding.

Leaving Helena that early, he could hope to make Wolverine a tad after noon. He started on the paint, leading the red bay, and they made good time in the crisp morning sunlight. Midway there Longarm paused on a windswept pine-covered rise—hence free of ticks—to take a crap off the trail a ways and change his saddle to the red bay before riding on.

As they headed down across an open vale, both ponies got a mite hard to handle in the ungrazed, almost stirrup-deep grass. He understood what was eating them. They wanted to eat some of that tempting grass.

Save for the imported and aptly named cheat grass you seldom saw, where the native grasses were healthy the Western breeds of grass grew slow but sure on deeper roots than the greener and hence more watery forage east of, say, Longitude 100. So such forage as Western wheat grass, little bluestem, buffalo grass, rice grass, or needle-and-thread packed almost as much nutrition as grain in their thicker water-thrifty stems and shorter blades. From the way stock acted, they likely tasted swell too. But Longarm heeled the red bay and gave a good jerk on the lead line, saying, "You were both watered and fed cracked corn this morning and we're in a hurry, damn it."

As they moved up the far slope he saw he'd only spoken for himself. He'd let them drink at the last side creek the trail crossed, but the love grass they were crossing now smelled so sweet it even tempted him to dismount and shove his fool face down in it. Love grass got its name because of the way stock loved it and because it made such swell sod for a picnic. Few schoolmarms reclining in love grass had a chance if their swain could keep them there after sundown and point out it never left grass stains, despite its sweet smell, no matter how hard you rubbed a summer skirt on it.

Near the top of the next rise, the love grass seemed even thicker, and he knew the little blue-stem mixed with it was teasing both ponies too. He muttered, half to himself, "Well, hell, fifteen minutes either way won't make or break us, and I can smoke in the shade of them lodgepoles yonder."

Then, suiting his actions to his words, he reined in and swung out of the saddle, almost in one graceful motion. So the rifle round aimed at the back of his denim jacket buzzed like an angry hornet past his startled nose instead, followed by the whip-crack report of the far-off saddle gun some son of a bitch had just fired.

Longarm let go of the pommel and cantle of his hornless army saddle, to land on his rump in the love grass and do a backward somersault before springing to his feet, six-gun in hand, to bolt for better cover than the two milling ponies.

He dove headfirst between two sprouting lodgepoles to somersault forward in more shady pine duff, sincerely glad he'd left his good tweed suit in his wardrobe back in Denver. The surface was dry. But the damper rotting needles you raked up by sincere sliding left tea-colored stains on sun-faded but hitherto fairly clean jeans.

Getting his duds dirty seemed the least of his worries as he got most of himself below the skyline on the far side and proceeded to scoot east, away from the Missouri, through the tall skinny pines. He knew his head might be visible as a rabbit-like movement from that next rise to the south. It couldn't be helped. He'd be in a worse fix if that dry-gulcher with a high-powered rifle broke his own cover before a man could circle clean around through the trees with a lousy .44–40 pissoliver!

The lodgepole-covered rises got closer together as one followed either back from the flood plain of the upper Missouri. Less than two miles on as the draw between rose higher, the trees grew clean across the saddle between and a man could run two miles really fast if he really needed to.

Longarm needed to, he saw, as he spotted movement across the way. He grunted, "Great minds run in the same channels," and now that he knew where that other cuss was, dropped further down the far side to start really picking them up and laying them down.

He had no way of knowing whether his secret admirer knew they were having a foot race along opposing pine ridges. He only knew he had to get well ahead of the bastard either way, so he just kept going as fast as he knew how.

That turned out fast enough as the long-legged and mighty winded Longarm gasped, "This must be the place!" and legged it up and over to see that, sure enough, there were trees ahead of him as he ran downhill for a swell change.

He hit bottom tearing between the skinny trunks and through the dappled shade with some gained momentum. Then, as he tore up the far slope with ever more painful strides, he spotted an outcrop of red sandstone surrounded by waist-high dwarf cedar and dropped into it, gasping for breath in the thin air but sliding an extra round in the wheel of his six-gun while he waited. For this seemed hardly the time to pack his side arm cautiously with only five in the wheel.

Aside from the greater range a rifle or carbine offered, Longarm knew the rascal had seven to sixteen rounds in his magazine, depending on what sort of repeater he was packing. Longarm had heard that flying lead from close enough to know it hadn't come from an older, heavier, and hence often single-shot hunting rifle.

He knew he'd outrun his man, possibly because it was easier to run with a pistol in one hand. He removed his hat and placed it on top of the outcrop he was forted behind. A few minutes later he made out movement amid the lodgepole trunks to the southwest. The cuss was moving at a cautious walk, proceeded by the muzzle of a Remington carbine he was pointing from the hip.

He pointed good. He'd no sooner spotted the hat atop the outcrop ahead of him than he fired and dropped, hitting Longarm's hat dead center as he wound up prone behind another clump of dwarf cedar.

Longarm called out, "Nice shooting, Santee. Now I'd like you to just leave that Remington where it is, unbuckle your gun belt, and follow your empty hands up where I can get a better look at you."

There came no answer.

Longarm insisted, "Give it up, Santee. I'm forted behind solid rock. That scrub you're pinned behind won't stop a determined horse fly. I'd rather take you in alive. We got a lot to talk about. But either way, I'm taking you in, Santee."

The gunslick behind the almost worthless cover fired. As his ricochet wailed off behind Longarm, the disgusted deputy let fly a couple of pistol rounds. He didn't buy that hat sailing skyward from the scrub at face value. He fired thrice more to make certain nobody was playing hat tricks on him. Then he reloaded, eased back, and made a wide circle through the trees till he could see just what he'd done.

He'd done the rascal good, he saw, moving closer to view the shot-up remains. The youthful figure sprawled across a blood-flecked long gun wore ragged-ass jeans and a once-blue shirt. It had been a paler blue than described. It was bloodstained considerably now. Longarm's fire had messed its owner up considerably too. Raking through the evergreen scrub, his five rounds had smashed down through both the dead kid's collarbones to rip out the small of his back at bloody angles, while that shot that had sent his dark Stetson flying had deposited blood, brain tissue, and hairy bits of skull down his back past the seat of his jeans.

Longarm holstered his .44–40 and got out a cheroot as he muttered, "I said I wanted to talk to you, damn it. Stick around while I find out if that gunplay left us stranded afoot out here in the middle of nowhere."

It hadn't. That yummy love grass had kept both of Longarm's ponies about where he'd last seen them. The dead kid had tethered his own buckskin to a lodgepole across the way before he'd commenced all the shooting. Longarm didn't find the change of mounts mysterious. Those bays he'd seen Dakota and Santee riding up the river were doubtless as jaded as the other ponies he and poor Bathsheba had been riding two days ago.

He led all three mounts back to where he'd left the dead kid. It took some tugging towards the last, when the three of them smelled death in the air. He tethered them closer than they'd wanted to go, and searched for his hat till he found it upside down in some tarweed. The fresh damage wouldn't be too noticeable once he had the poor hat cleaned and blocked back in Denver. Between all the trail dust and the more recent sticky stains from that tarweed, the old J.B. could use both.

He got the dead kid across his own roping saddle facedown. It wasn't easy. He had to really hurt the buckskin with the bit before he was done. It calmed some once he had the body securely lashed down with latigo leathers and tied the buckskin on short rein to the way longer lead line so it could follow between the red bay and the steadier paint.

They moved on, cutting cross-country till they rejoined the trail a couple of furlongs east of the flood line of the Big Muddy River to their west.

The next few hours passed without much incident, save for the odd colors a man's face turned, hanging head down as lividity and rigor mortis commenced to set in. There was a heap of common sense as well as consideration in the almost universal tradition calling for dead folks to be placed on their backs with their hands folded across their chests. Hands and faces looked far nicer going sort of waxy as blood corpuscles slowly settled, the way milk separates from cream after a stationary spell. But shit, it wasn't as if a man owed any favors to a son of a bitch who'd just tried to back-shoot him, and it would have been a bitch to ride the cadaver all the way to town faceup.

So the kid he had down as the late Santee was all purple-faced and pouty-lipped by the time they met up with some cowhands branding a maverick yearling in another draw way closer to town. Longarm had pinned his badge to the front of his jacket right after lashing the dead kid across his saddle with just such meetings in mind. But one of the hands, on his side of their fire, recognized him from around Wolverine and hailed him, asking, "Who shot old Top Hand there, Deputy Long?"

As all but the hand holding the maverick down moved to meet him, mounted or afoot, Longarm called back, "Me. I had to. He was aiming a Remington repeater at me. But who might we be talking about? Ain't this a saddle bum called Santee I've been hauling all over creation?"

The local rider who knew him moved closer afoot for a closer look before he insisted, "That's Top Hand MacTaggert you got there. The nickname was meant sarcastic. If he'd had more brains he might have qualified as our village idiot. No outfit would hire a poor cuss who couldn't rope a hitching post if someone held it still for him!"

A laconic rider on a nearby dun volunteered, "Lived mostly as an errand boy around Wolverine. Lord knows where he got that pony and them guns. He kept *trying* to say he was a serious rider, but like Slim says, nobody would hire him for anything more serious than, say, swamping out a saloon under close supervision."

The one called Slim said, "He tried to join up with Les Kenmore's vigilance committee. But they wouldn't take him. He offered to deputy for Sheriff Wallward, but they had no use for him neither."

Longarm glanced back at the facedown body thoughtfully as he said, "I had him down as someone else entirely, and say what you will about him, he was a pretty good shot. So somebody sure found use for him more recent than the folks you mentioned."

Chapter 11

Riding into Wolverine that afternoon with a local boy who'd made bad created more of a sensation. Kids old and young, along with a yellow dog, tagged after Longarm till he reined in out front of the sheriff's office and deposited the remains on the steps faceup, although hardly unbent all the way and really starting to look ugly.

As Walt Wallward and two deputies came out, they were joined by most of the men and at least half the women and children in town. A hatchet-faced gent Longarm recognized as Edward Skane, the former lawman who ran the general store down the way, declared without hesitation, "That's Tavish MacTaggert. They called him Top Hand in jest. He was a simpleton I sometimes hired to run errands for us."

Longarm replied, "So I've been told. I may want to talk with you about other matters as well later, Mister Skane."

The storekeeper nodded in an easygoing way and said, "Any time. Come for supper, if you like."

Walt Wallward cut in. "We all know who the kid was, Longarm. How did he wind up missing the top of his fool skull?"

Longarm said, "I cannot tell a lie. I did it with my little

.44–40, and you were all right about him being stupid. He was forted up in dwarf cedar twigs in the apparent conviction they could stop bullets. Before that he was trying to put bullets in *me*. I reckon a cuss who'd swamp saloons and deliver groceries would do most anything for a buck."

There came a murmur of agreement from the crowd all around when their sheriff declared, "I'd have never thought he had it in him! I'd seen the boy shoot. He practiced all the time with a muzzle-loading squirrel rifle, and it was about the only thing he was any good at. Where was he laying for you, out of town beyond earshot?"

Longarm pointed at the buckskin pony and replied, "Way out of town, aboard yonder roping saddle. He had that Remington you see riding in its saddle boot, and we're in total agreement about his marksmanship. I don't suppose anybody here has ever seen that buckskin pony before either?"

The sheriff said, "You suppose wrong. I'm pretty sure that mount was with the stock we brought in from that so-called Tall Tom's so-called placer claim."

He turned to one of his deputies to ask, "Jim?"

The younger lawman said, "Sure looks like one of Plowright's ponies. Only it's supposed to be over in the livery paddock, grazing with the others."

An old bearded gent in bib overalls piped up, "Don't you dare go saying I've been hiring rides to paid assassins, Jim Booker! If that's one of the critters you asked us to board for you while you're holding its owner, that MacTaggert kid must had borrowed it unauthorized. As I study back, Top Hand did do some haying chores for us this morning. But we never told him he could borrow any riding stock to go shooting at folks with!"

Longarm suggested they trot the de facto owner of the buckskin out front to see if he could shed any light on the mystery.

145

Walt Wallward said he'd been about to say the same thing, and sent his deputies in to fetch the prisoner.

The tall, lantern-jawed, and scar-faced mystery man hadn't changed his story since they'd had him locked up in the back. He was repeating his innocence as they led him out front hatless, coatless, and with his hands cuffed in front of him. He seemed genuinely surprised to see the dead youth, and readily admitted he knew Top Hand MacTaggert. He said, "The kid did some shoveling for me early on. I had to let him go because he dropped more placer back in the creek than he did in my sluice."

Ed Skane said that sure sounded like they were talking about the same fool kid. The sheriff growled, "Mebbe. If I thought for even one minute this yahoo was running a real placer operation up yonder!"

The mystery man calling himself Plowright protested, "What I do on my own mining claim is my own business, Sheriff! If you're trying to accuse me of killing this boy, or sending him out to be killed, I would like to remind you I've been locked up in your vile jail for almost forty-eight hours without a chance to speak to anyone! Need I add this is unconstitutional as well?"

Walt Wallward shot Longarm a worried look, saying, "He may just have us, pard. None of us ever told him where you were headed or when you might be back. We'd have noticed if that dead boy on my steps had been visiting with him inside, and we're either going to have to book him and let him see a lawyer, or let him go once we've held him three whole days."

Longarm said, "I know. We'd best book him and let him talk to all the lawyers he wants. I don't see how any lawyer in these parts can defend him once Canada extradites him. Murder cum rape are serious charges, and that Yankee-hating Prime Minister MacDonald up Canada way ain't about to let anyone but a member of the Canadian bar try a case in any Canadian court."

The prisoner wasn't the only one there who seemed surprised by Longarm's announcement. The sheriff demanded, "You say Canada has a warrant out on Thomas Plowright for murder or rape?"

Longarm said, "Both. They suspect he's the same villain who choked a missionary to the Cree to death as he was having his wicked ways with her fair white body. My Mountie pal, Crown Sergeant Foster, has another name entirely on the disgusting rascal. But how many lantern-jawed and scarfaced giants might there be out our way wandering all over under made-up names?"

The man insisting his name was Plowright wailed, "I've never done anything bad to any Canadian ladies! I've never even been up Canada way. I was born and bred near Elkton, Maryland—before me and my brothers moved out to Ohio, I mean!"

"That ain't what Ohio said when I wired there about the Plowright tribe as well," said Longarm dryly. Then he shrugged. "Why don't we just put him back in his cell to await the pleasure of Her Majesty Queen Victoria or that Yankee-hating Canadian government she's got up yonder? We don't have to prove spit, one way or the other, now that we'll soon be rid of the rascal no matter who he really is."

Walt Wallward brightened, laughed, and said, "I follow your drift. Take this rascal back to his cell, boys."

As his deputies started to do so the tall mystery man protested, "Hold on! This isn't fair! Nobody ever said anything about Canadian charges against the Plowright boys. I mean, *us* Plowright boys. I want that lawyer. We need to study more on this, Sheriff!"

Wallward said, "Take him away," and as they did so turned to Longarm with a chuckle to say, softer, "What'll you bet he changes his story a heap before morning?"

Longarm said, "I figure before midnight. Why don't we give him that long to sweat, and then start going through the bullshit of booking him formal?"

The sheriff agreed that sounded like fun, and added, "It ain't for me to say. But I'm sure the coroner's jury will find this fool kid committed suicide by ill-advised gunplay."

Then he stared blankly around and asked, "Say, where *is* the doc this afternoon? I see we got most everyone else out here by now."

Ed Skane said, "I think he rode out to the Widow Andrews' spread to treat a spavined brood mare. But speaking as a member of his usual panel, I'd say you were right about MacTaggert's dumb death. Meanwhile, it might be a good idea to store him somewhere cooler than them sunny steps till we can hold a meeting and formalize his demise."

The sheriff said his boys could carry the remains to a nearby root cellar and rustle up some rock salt. So Longarm gave the pony the kid had been riding back to the livery manager and took the others around to the back.

He put them in with the rest of the remuda. He was storing his saddle and bridle in the tack shed when Sheriff Wallward caught up with him, saying, "I sent one of my boys out to the Andrews spread. We'll know soon enough when the doc wants to take your formal statement. I mean to save myself some paperwork by simply filing a copy of the coroner's findings. What do you suppose got into that backward young cuss anyhow?"

Longarm shrugged as he got some spare cheroots and ammunition out of a saddlebag. "Bad company. Some slicker talker had noticed that despite his other faults the kid was a pretty good shot. I ain't sure how they put it to him without hurting his feelings, but we both know he'd have been about the last cuss anyone would have suspected if he'd left me dead along the trail from Helena."

Wallward nodded soberly. "I follow your drift. You'd told everybody about your earlier run in with the brighter-acting ones called Dakota and . . . what's his name?"

Longarm said, "Santee. His pal, Dakota, is no longer with us, by the way. I forgot to announce it out front on purpose, but it looks like Santee or some other owlhoot rider gunned Dakota the other night in Helena. They're still working on whether it was an accident or to shut him up."

The older lawman whistled softly. "Somebody's sure been playing rough. How come you don't want nobody out front to know?"

Then, before Longarm could answer, Wallward nodded and said, "Oh, sure, nobody in town but you, me, and may-haps some mastermind would know unless you told 'em. So you want to see who might know without you telling 'em!"

Longarm nodded but warned, "Don't be too hasty if some-body seems to slip. I know there's no telegraph here in Wolverine, but I might not have been the only rider who ever rode that trail. So knowing a mite more about events in Helena has to be treated as a sign, not proof."

Walward grumbled that he knew how to conduct a proper investigation, and asked where Longarm was headed next.

Longarm replied, "Investigating, of course. The saloon gossip ought to be starting early this afternoon, and I might need me a shave and a haircut at the barbershop down the way now that I've had time to study on my shabby appear-ance. The son of a bitch behind all this has managed to hide who he is by hiding his infernal motive for all his deadly bullshit. But there has to be a motive, unless he's just a homicidal lunatic, and they don't work in bunches."

Wallward followed him outside, saying, "I've been try-ing to make sense of what my secret enemy could be after since before you got here. For the life of me I can't see what he expects to gain by all this deadly but pointless misbehavior! I mean, wouldn't it make more sense for my secret enemy to just have me dry-gulched right off before you, Billy Vail, or even poor old Silas Mullens knew I had any secret enemy?"

Longarm said, "Yep. Shaving with Ockham's Razor seems to show you couldn't be the object of our mastermind's affection. Being the law, you may be considered an obstacle to be gotten around, with the help of some misdirection. That's what stage magicians call it when they get you to look the wrong way whilst they're pulling something else."

"Pulling what?" asked Walward in a sincerely puzzled tone.

To which Longarm could only reply, "I ain't sure. I can only hope someone who might know might make a slip. I'm starting at the saloon just up the way. You coming, Walt?"

The older lawman smiled wistfully and replied, "You know why I try to avoid saloons, old son. I'd best ask my own questions up and down the creek, and we'll talk about it at supper time. You will be supping with us this evening, right?"

Longarm said, "I'd like to. I can't. Ed Skane invited me over to his place for supper, and no offense to Miss Flo's cooking, I'd like to hear more about his wild and woolly days in the Indian Nation."

The incumbent sheriff looked disgusted. "He told you how he cleaned up the Cherokee Strip before I ever wore a badge, did he?"

Longarm shook his head. "Nope. Learned he was supposed to be a former federal deputy when I was in Helena. Ain't heard anything about it from Skane yet. Have you heard the Grangers wanted to run him against you come the fall elections?"

Wallward grimaced. "I figured it was Lester Kenmore, but it don't surprise me. Nothing those loco Grangers might be planning comes as any great surprise to me no more. Stockmen and farmers who want to lower the value of the U.S. dollar and raise the taxes on all landholdings can't be playing with a full deck!"

Longarm said he doubted the Granger Movement would ever get too far either, and they split up out front to go their separate ways.

Longarm only had one beer and some pointless conversation in the Big Belt Saloon. He never went to the barber down the other way at all. He ambled casually along that side of the creek until he got to Edward Skane's general store.

Inside, he found the hatchet-faced older man waiting on a lady customer. A perky gal in her teens moved down the counter to ask if she could please Longarm in any manner. Aside from her looking way too young, her dad was standing there in plain sight. So he told Skane's daughter, knowing Skane could hear, he was a federal lawman there on federal business.

Skane asked his perky kid if she'd help Widow Blane pick out some yard goods, and led Longarm into the back storeroom where they could talk more privately. When Longarm asked where Skane's family quarters might be, the storekeeper said, "Across the yard out back. Why?"

Longarm said, "I'm taking you up on that invite to supper. I've let it be known all up and down the street out front."

Skane started to object, shrugged, and replied with a sheepish smile, "That's right. I *did* say you were welcome to stay for supper. But to tell the truth . . . I'd best run back and tell the wife to put more spuds in her oven."

Longarm shook his head and said, "In a minute. I can't make you do this, Deputy Skane. But I'd sure like you to send your family off to sup somewhere safer whilst you and me set up a trap. I have to warn you, as a man with more to lose than me, that it might turn out sort of noisy. I was invited to supper by Silas Mullens that evening I'm sure you remember all too well."

Skane stared thunderstruck. "You mean it was you, not anyone else at the table, they were out to kill with that infernal device?"

Longarm nodded soberly. "I didn't know for certain till they made another more desperate try for me personally out on the trail where I was the only possible target."

Skane hesitated, then said, "My wife and the girls ought to be safe enough at her sister's place, a quarter mile out of town. My two boys would never forgive me if I didn't let them back our play. My Rob is pushing twenty and Sandy is almost eighteen."

Longarm started to object. Then he nodded soberly and softly told the older man, "I was about that age when I run off to join an army one time, and you're right, the fool kids would never forgive you if you told them they couldn't fight beside us."

The clouds above were starting to blush pink by the time Rob Skane got back from his Aunt Ruth's spread afoot and scaled the ladder propped between the general store and the next-door notions shop. As his kid brother helped him up on the flat roof he called out, "Don't reckon nobody saw us when I snuck Mom and the girls out of town and moseyed back through the trees like you said, Dad."

His father, prone beside Longarm near the back parapet of the flat tar-paper roof, called back softly, "Keep your voices down, damn it. Sandy, show him where his Yellowboy is and then take up your own position behind our false front to the east."

As the two denim-clad youths spread out, one armed with

an antique repeating Spencer, the other covering his own field of fire with the early-model Winchester or Yellowboy, Longarm and the owner of all this endangered property lay side by side a few yards apart to cover the backyard and the tidy little cottage. Its dining room window was smiling through lace curtains with all those penny candles Slade had just lit atop a deserted supper table. It looked as if someone was about to sup in there to Longarm, as had been his plan from the beginning.

Skane, drawing on his own experiences in the Indian Nation, asked, "What if someone sneaks in the back way through the trees, as Rob just did?"

Longarm said calmly, "Let's hope so. The rascal would be less likely to spot us up here with that false front raised against the sky behind us. But they never lobbed any bomb through the Mullens' back windows. You got to remember that if they come at all they won't be after you or your kin. They'll be out to spoil *my* supper, and there's no way to lob anything through your dining room window yonder without us seeing 'em. Your boys will see 'em sooner if they come along the street either way with a lit bundle of dynamite."

Skane said that sounded sort of wild. Longarm shrugged and said, "The whole thing's been wild from the beginning. We figure they hit and run on horseback at the Mullens place the other night."

In the time they'd been setting up, the older man with some federal training had gotten the whole story, or as much of it as Longarm knew. So he found it easy to say that the brains behind all the recent trouble had to be warped as hell.

Longarm said, "Top Hand MacTaggert might have been a half-wit. But the ones called Dakota, Santee, and even that spooky Tall Tom we've got locked away talked as if they had average sense. Gents of any sense don't follow orders from a raving maniac who can't offer a sensible reason for anything he wants them to do."

Skane complained, "I'll be damned if I can make sense out of a thing they've done. Why would Dakota and Santee pick a fight with you when you first got up this way, and then back off, as if to let you know they were after you, before they were ready to come after you sincerely?"

Longarm suggested, "They wanted other lawmen, not me, to know two fictitious characters called Dakota and Santee were after me. I've compared notes by wire with lawmen all over, and nobody nowhere has any warrants or yellow sheets on such a menacing team."

Skane nodded soberly. "Real gunslicks working together for any time under those handles would have surely left some record of their wanderings. But Walt Wallward couldn't be holding that big scar-faced cuss right now if you hadn't found something on him. So what was it, aside from impersonating a dead man?"

Longarm chuckled and replied, "That ain't no felony, as well he knew, or was told, when someone noticed his vague resemblance to a cuss killed long ago and no longer wanted anywhere. I told Walt he was wanted more seriously up Canada way."

Skane asked what the tall stranger had done in Canada. So Longarm smiled thinly and admitted, "Nothing, far as I know. But you can't hold a suspect the usual seventy-two on nothing. So I made something up."

The former lawman chuckled. "We used to do that over to Fort Smith from time to time. A whiskey trader locked away on a robbery charge can sure talk careless about his sour mash in the woods whilst trying to prove he was nowhere near the robbery in question. But do you and Walt expect any man with the brains of a gnat to confess to real crimes to get out of standing trial for something he knows nobody can prove?"

Longarm shrugged and shifted his Winchester to cover the backyard more thoughtfully as he replied, "We don't know what kind of brains he has. He's already going around telling folks he's a dead man. Meanwhile, holding him in the county lockup ought to worry his pals two ways. He sure as shit can't carry out any orders for anybody, and there's always that one chance in a hundred he'll talk. I suspect he was recruited only to put on that menacing act for some reason. If he never took part in anything more serious, he may tell us the reason."

Skane thought and said, "That's right. He's got perfect alibis for the murder of Dakota and that attempt to dry-gulch you whilst he was locked up all the while!"

Longarm said, "He has a perfect alibi for the bombing of Silas Mullens and those other poor souls too. Ain't it a good thing I was smart enough to connect him with a murder-rape north of the border?"

Before Skane could answer his younger boy, Sandy, hissed, "Rider coming in from the west and, Jesus, that looks like a lit fuse he's waving from his free hand!"

Longarm had just snapped, "Aim for his pony!" when the rattled but straight-shooting youth let fly with his Spencer and said "Oops!"

Then Longarm was on his feet and tearing across the tar paper to join Sandy Skane as, out on the street, a figure dimly outlined by the rudy sunset landed flat on his back in a cloud of dust while his bay pony just kept going. Then came a brilliant orange fireball and a horrendous roar, and Longarm could thank his stars he'd landed on his ass atop the general store before the shock wave had sent him over the far side.

He lay there, staring up at the flame and purple sky as glass tinkled down all around while doors and shattered windows crashed open all over town. Then he rolled over, dragged his Winchester after him to the ladder, and slid down it to join the gathering crowd out front. A woman had already fainted and strong men were turning away to retch as Longarm elbowed through to view what Sandy Skane had done with one well-placed rifle round.

The dynamite the fallen rider had been packing had done the rest. There was a broad shallow crater in the street with bits and pieces of bloody rags and gobs of flesh strewn all around. Two spurred boots with blood oozing out of them were larger and more easy to identify than anything else, until a townsman drifted in with a dove-gray J.B. to announce, "I think the poor cuss must have been wearing this. It has some of his skull stuck to the crown inside."

Longarm nudged a bloody dress-blue rag with a boot tip as he said, "If this was part of his shirt he called himself Santee. The bay pony I caught a glimpse of says the same. Maybe there'll be something in its saddlebags we can use, if ever it stops running up the creek."

Sheriff Wallward came bulling through the crowd to join him gasping, "Thunderation, that was noisy! Cracked a window in the front of my office way down yonder. You say that there is the cuss called Santee?"

Longarm said, "What's left of him. He was out to heave dynamite through a window at suppertime again. I figured he might. Got Ed Skane and his boys to help me set up a trap this time."

He saw young Sandy pushing through the crowd with his Spencer, and Longarm had been a kid once as well. But it was also meant for his proud-looking dad, just behind Sandy, when Longarm said in a louder tone, "It was Sandy Skane as dropped the murderous rascal with as fine a single rifle shot as ever you did see!"

As the crowd murmured the expected approval, the sheriff was sport enough to nod at the son of his Granger rival and say, "The whole county owes you, Sandy. No telling who the maniac might have blown up if you hadn't stopped him."

The kid dug the toe of one boot in the dust and blushed like a schoolmarm who'd been told she was pretty.

Longarm told the sheriff in a softer tone, "Don't think Santee was a maniac. Doubt his real name was Santee. He was hired to act menacing and then, when that didn't work, the mastermind who hired him gave him heavier chores to carry out."

"To what end?" the sheriff murmured back. "Even if they'd scared us worse than they did with all that menacing shit, what in blue blazes were they trying to get us to *do*?"

Longarm suggested, "Let's go ask the tall one we've got locked up and sweating. He ought to know and with any luck he's sweat enough by now."

The sheriff said, "You go ahead, and if you see any of my boys send them up this way, will you? You'll find the prisoner in that same cell and the keys are in my desk out front. Meanwhile, I can't just let this mess lay spread all over the street till the hogs get at it."

Longarm nodded and eased away through the crowd, wishing nobody had reminded him of free-ranging hogs before he'd ever had his damn supper that evening. it had been quite a spell after the war before he could enjoy pork chops without thinking back to many a battlefield and the way all too many bodies had been disposed of by hogs, dogs, eye-pecking crow birds—and the biggest rats he'd ever seen amid the trenches around Petersburg.

There was nobody on the street down by the sheriff's office. He noted the cracked window Walt had mentioned and went inside. Thanks to the fading daylight outside it was about lamp-lighting time. But no lamps had been lit in the empty front office. Longarm called out, got no answer, and lit a desk lamp as well as a fresh cheroot before he found a big key ring in one of the desk drawers and headed back to the gloomy cells, smiling thinly as he speculated, "He must be sort of hungry as well as tired of pacing back and forth in the gloom."

As he barely made out the tall figure facing his way against the bars he cheerfully called out, "That blast you likely heard was your pal Santee getting blown to bits. As you can see, he failed again to spoil my supper. But I'm hungry as hell. How about you?"

The man who called himself Plowright didn't answer. Longarm put an experimental key in the lock, muttering, "Strong silent type, eh? Well, nobody can say you ain't big. So let's work on whether you're big and dumb."

The first key didn't work. A second one did, and Longarm swung the cell door open, saying, "Let's go. I'm taking you to supper at the Big Belt whilst we have a serious discussion about all this shit."

The taller figure, the much taller figure, didn't answer. The hairs on the back of Longarm's neck commenced to tingle as he got out a match to thumbnail some light on the subject.

The first thing he noticed by the flickering matchlight was the way the prisoner's boot tips cleared the floor by a good four inches. The noose of dark braided leather was tougher to make out as he held the light up to the giant's scarred face. It was tied to a top cross-bar of the cage-like front of the cell, with the loop dug into the flesh of the prisoner's throat under the lantern jaw. So it was no wonder he seemed to be standing smack against the bars like that.

The strangled giant's big rawboned hands had not been bound. So it was easy to feel in vain for a pulse. Once he was sure the cuss was sincerely dead, Longarm muttered, "Well, you won't feel a flea's fart better if I cut you down, and that new scientific detecting they write about in the French and English newpapers makes mention of not messing up the scene of the crime till everyone's had time to study it thoroughly."

He took a thoughtful drag on his cheroot, nodded, and told the dead man, "You'd best just hang around whilst I go fetch the sheriff. Mayhaps he can help me figure out whether the crime here was a murder or a suicide. As you likely knew as you were dying, on the face of the evidence, it works as well either way!"

Chapter 12

An ashen-faced Walt Wallward, on viewing the evidence for himself, favored suicide, saying, "He was alive and well, albeit sobbing some back here, when I heard that explosion and tore up the street to see what had happened."

Pointing at the dangling hands of the hanging cadaver, Wallward added, "You can see he was free to put up a struggle, and how many bigger and stronger men could there be in Montana Territory?"

Longarm suggested, "Two could have held him whilst another choked him with that braided leather. Once they had him unconscious it would have been no great chore to tie the other end up yonder and let him dangle. I see the leather stretched some. Where do you reckon it came from, Walt?"

The sheriff sighed and said, "From around his waist. I know we're supposed to take belts, neckties, and shoelaces away from them, but he said his pants were loose and, shit, how was I to know he was out to kill himself? I thought he was after *me*!"

Longarm said, "Let's consider the time all concerned had to work with. I agree a prisoner with a worried mind had plenty of time to hang his fool self after you tore out the front to leave him and his belt unguarded back here."

The sheriff protested, "Damn it, old son, my deputies have to eat their own suppers, and what was I supposed to do when enough dynamite went off outside to wake the dead?"

Longarm nodded and said, "Running up the street to join the crowd was just what anyone would expect you to do. But I agree it would call for brass balls and hairy timing by someone who knew in advance what was fixing to happen."

Wallward asked, "You mean they set off that blast as a ruse, just to get at this fake Plowright?"

Longarm shrugged. "They must have been after me as well. That makes even less sense. Why would they kill another pal to keep me from making him talk if they were planning to kill me in the first place?"

The older lawman grumbled, "Thanks a heap. I reckon you don't think I could get a confession out of a prisoner after his pals had blown up my star pupil and gotten me *really* vexed with 'em!"

Longarm smiled sheepishly and admitted, "There I go pretending it's my personal cockle-doodle-doo that makes the sun rise every morning. You're right. They figured you and your boys would question this cuss Ranger-style once they'd done me in. So now we know this tall drink of water knew everything that was going on."

"Unless he was just loco," the sheriff said, pointing the other way. "Say they knew that dynamite would go off. Say they knew I'd tear off like a damn fool instead of sending somebody. Say they knew where I kept my keys, knew my prisoner was wearing the right sort of belt to hang him with, and then say the two or more it would have taken got in and out without being spotted."

Longarm said, "We won't know nobody spotted them before we canvas the neighborhood. Somebody who only

161

saw two or more figures enter and leave by your front door, in tricky light, would have no good reason to come forward without being asked."

The older lawman brightened. "You're right. Soon as my night men get back from supper I'll leave one in charge here and the rest of us can get right on it."

Longarm said, "I'd as soon start now. Unless you're afraid of staying by yourself with a corpse."

Wallward snorted in derision, but said, "I'd be obliged if you'd send any of my deputies you meet to give me a hand here, though. At the rate we're going we'll have more bodies than the coroner can shake a stick at before he ever makes it back to town!"

Longarm agreed and headed out to the street. As he opened the front door he almost wound up with a meat pie stuck to his chest. Flo Wallward, the sheriff's gimpy but still handsome wife, pulled back just in time with the tray in her hand, saying, "You startled me. I just heard about that horrible death up the street and so, knowing Walter and the rest of you might not be able to manage a sit-down supper, I thought . . ."

"You don't want to go back there, ma'am," Longarm told her, taking the tray gently but firmly from her as she started to move around him in the doorway.

When she asked why, he said, "It ain't pretty. I'm sure Walt wouldn't want you to see it. I'll put this swell meat pie and coffee on yonder desk and fetch him, ma'am. But you'd best stay right where you are."

She followed, insisting, "Not unless you tell me what this is all about, Custis!"

So he turned back, tray in hand, and said, "That prisoner who said he was a dead man is dead. It was me as found him, hanging in his cell. I was on my way to fetch help. Masculine help, no offense. Why don't you go on around back and I'll tell Walt you was here with his coffee and grub, hear?"

But as he moved to put the tray atop the desk she limped after him, asking, "Please tell me, Custis, who do you suspect of trying so hard to make my man look bad?"

He turned back to take her by one elbow and gently steer her toward the front door as he confided, "I got more suspects than I have motives, Miss Flo. Why do you say all this menacing has been to make your man look bad?"

She turned in the doorway to fix him with an intelligent smile and say, "Oh, come now, you've surely wondered about a man who seems too befuddled to say for certain an obvious lunatic can't be an outlaw he shot himself years ago."

Longarm smiled back. "The thought occurred to me when first I was told my old mentor needed my help with a haunt. But I got to meet the cuss who said he was Tall Tom Plowright, and whilst he can't say so now, he told me in front of witnesses he was the same Thomas Plowright Walt and I rode after seven years ago. So, no, I can't say your man looks loco or even more confused than me."

She said softly, "Some people are starting to talk about how good we must have felt when our main political enemy, Silas Mullens, was blown up that way the other night. I know they were really after you, but it was Silas Mullens printing all those dreadful things about my Walter being a liar about his earlier days as a lawman, and is it true that other explosion this evening was aimed to blow up the man the Grangers are *really* running for sheriff this fall?"

Longarm said gently, "Silas Mullens was never fixing to run for anything, and Ed Skane ain't made his mind up yet. I follow your drift as far as some killings or attempted killings, ma'am. But they've been trying as hard or harder to kill me and I'm on Walt's side. Have been from the beginning.

So anybody killing me would make Walt's political foes look suspicious and then where would they be, if that was anyone's true reason?"

She seemed to feel better as he got her outside, ducked back in, and yelled, "Hey, Walt? There's coffee and grub out here!" before he went out on the dark street himself.

He went up to the Big Belt and, sure enough, they were willing to whip up corned-beef-on-rye sandwiches for a customer who needled his beer with four bits worth of brand-name whiskey. But none of the after-supper crowd recalled anyone dashing in or out of the sheriff's office as they'd all dashed up the street to see what had blown out all that window glass.

He wrangled another sandwich, this one pickles and cheese, and did more tedious legwork along the unlit street. It saved him some time, but did him no good, to note that most of the businesses facing the street with even a half-ass view of the sheriff's front door were shut down for the night. When he asked at another saloon he was told most would have been closed for supper by the time of the blast.

Moving on in the ever-darker gloom, he spied a bay cow pony lit up somewhat better by the lamplight beaming through the frosted glass windows of yet a third saloon, almost up to Ed Skane's place.

He paused to have a better look at the tethered pony. It didn't tell him much. Had it been the bay bolting out from under the shot-up Santee, somebody would have brought it down to the sheriff, not to this dinky saloon. But he went on in anyway, having no place better to ask questions. The place wasn't crowded at that hour despite being little more than a hole in the wall. By this time he knew most of the boys around Wolverine on sight. The young slim cuss drinking alone at the far end, near a silent piano against the far wall, went best with the cow pony outside. Townsmen tended to leave their mounts at home when they strolled over to their neighborhood saloon. The stranger was dressed more for the range as well. His hat was a tan Carlsbad and his shirt was neither buckskin nor army dress blue. But he sure favored big spur rowels and heaps of silver fittings on his tooled side-draw gun rig. His gun, as well as Longarm could make out from little more than the tailored grips, was a Harrington Richardson double-action of any caliber. The well-heeled rider was nursing a big but nearly full scuttle of suds, as if waiting for someone or something. Those hairs were rising on the back of Longarm's neck again, but you couldn't go up to a gent who wasn't doing anything and ask what he was doing, without looking like someone who'd been packing a badge too long.

Hickok had whirled on one heel to gun his own pal, Mike Williams, in an Abilene gunfight. But then, possibly afraid he was getting too quick on the trigger, he'd let a blowhard like Cockeyed Jack McCall work around behind him in that Deadwood saloon. So the idea was to keep a sense of balance between to draw or not to draw.

Nodding at everyone down the bar as if he knew them all, Longarm bellied up and braced one boot on the brass rail, with his gun grips a tad close to the wood but his eyes on the mirror of the back-bar as he allowed he'd have a schooner of plain draft. As the barkeep got him set up he fumbled out some change, muttering, "Hey, I ain't had that much to drink yet," and placed it on the zinc top. The barkeep naturally addressed him by name and asked if they'd found out any more about that cuss blown to bits just up the street. Longarm lifted the schooner left-handed to sip some suds before he replied, "Coroner ain't back yet far as I know. I've been up and down in other places, as you can see, asking if anyone in town saw doodly shit. So far, all I've been getting is drunk. You don't serve any food in here, do you? Black coffee will do if your kitchen's closed. I don't want to come in walking funny if they do call a coroner's hearing tonight."

The barkeep said they could fix him up with a sandwich and some coffee, both cold, and headed back to a beaded curtain at the rear. As he passed the lone drinker down that way, the stranger wearing the Carlsbad pushed away from the bar and headed Longarm's way, slow and thoughtful. Longarm rolled halfway round, his gun hand free but his gun grips in an awkward position against the bar, as he nodded in a friendly way and said, "Evening, Santee."

It worked. An innocent cowhand who didn't know what he was talking would have said so and received a handsome apology. But a guilty man with guilty knowledge saw the best chance he was ever likely to have with a lawman of Longarm's rep and took it, going for the tailored grips of the double-action in his quick-draw rig in the certainty no man born of mortal woman was going to get an awkwardly positioned gun from a cross-draw rig any faster!

He was right, of course. He'd have killed Longarm for certain if an older and wiser gunfighter hadn't palmed his double derringer during the charade of fumbling out that change.

So the desperate sneak was dead on his feet, going back like a sawn-through pine on his locked knees, with his gun hand still in place on the tailored grips of his holstered six-gun as Longarm let his discharged derringer fall to the saw-dust while he whipped out his more serious side arm.

The barkeep ran back in, yelling, "Who fired them shots?" before he saw what lay spread like a bear rug across his floor. Then he gulped and added, "I reckon it's all right, seeing it was you, Deputy Long!"

A less sober gent on Longarm's side of the bar decided, "That was the fastest draw I ever saw. You had two rounds in him before you had your gun out. Who was the suicidal lunatic, Uncle Sam?"

Longarm said soberly, "You just heard him answer to the handle I tried on him. Lord only knows how many Santees there were to start with. I kept forgetting how easy it was to fool a man with ringers when he didn't really know anyone all that well and . . . Jesus, that has to be *it* and forget what I said about fools. They've been making a total asshole out of me!"

The county deputy called Jim tore in, gun drawn, to slide to a halt, take in the scene, and decide, "Oh, it was you and I see you got another one of 'em. Sheriff Wallward already had us out looking for you, Longarm. The doc got back after having supper out at the Andrews spread. So they were fixing to have a coroner's hearing at the Big Belt. But I see you got another death to be explained up this way!"

Longarm holstered his unfired six-gun and bent to scoop up his empty derringer, saying, "I'd best go down and explain a whole lot of things whilst everyone's in one place. Do you reckon you could get some help and haul this cadaver down to the hearing, Jim? He goes with the one we found hanging and the parts Walt had you boys gather up in that milk bucket earlier."

Jim said he'd be proud to assist in the investigation. So Longarm left, reloading his derringer and snapping it back on one end of his watch chain as he strode down the dark walk, feeling stupid even as he ran everything through his mind again to make sure he had all the hitherto disconnected facts connected sensibly. He thought of a few less important angles he could slice off and forget with old William of Ockham's razor. Who'd changed hats with whom, and why, didn't seem to really matter, once you decided to forget deliberate razzle-dazzle. Nobody would ever know for certain, and that old pirate who'd said dead men told no tales had been on the money.

He moseyed up to the window light from the Big Belt Saloon and saw they'd set up more formally there than they had in the wreckage of the *Wolverine Free Press*. But this rustic coroner was content with a single card table out front, where a good crowd could watch him do his stuff.

A good-sized crowd had gathered. When Longarm asked a town deputy near the swinging doors, it transpired all the dead meat had been left in that root cellar, where it wouldn't make gents sick as they tried to decide the causes of death.

Walt Wallward was against the bar near the coroner's table, not drinking. As he nodded a greeting the old horse doctor called out, "We've been waiting on you, Longarm. Can you shed any light on those two shots we just heard somewhere in the night?"

Longarm said, "Yep. I fired both. I had to. I was face to face with the real Santee. Or the crew leader who called himself Santee, I mean. The one Sandy Skane there shot was likely another would-be desperado recruited from amid your own wayward youths. You ought to be able to identify that bucket of body parts once its mamma reports her sensitive child missing."

The sheriff leaned away from the bar, saying he'd best take a look and asking where Longarm had shot it out with the mysterious Santee.

Longarm said, "Stick around. It's about to get more interesting and your deputy, Jim, has a handle on things up yonder."

The sheriff stayed put, with a puzzled frown, and asked what could be more interesting than a gunfight with a killer.

Longarm drifted closer to the coroner's table to get most of the crowd out of his line of fire as he replied, "I'm hoping to avoid another one, but you just never know."

Then he announced, "I want everyone here to stay put and stay out of it whilst I do me some arresting around here!"

The sheriff gasped, "You aim to arrest someone in this very taproom, old son?"

Longarm nodded and mildly asked, "Don't you reckon it's about time? You know what Abe Lincoln said about fooling all of the people all of the time."

Their eyes locked, and once again in less than an hour Longarm had that old and all too familiar feeling of weary disgust intermingled with cold fear as he somehow knew this was it.

He tried anyway. He softly said, "I suspect I know what you're thinking and you'd better think again. This is real life and stage acting ain't about to cut the mustard."

He saw the hesitation in the other man's eyes as the crowded taproom fell silent as the tomb. Despite all the mythology about quick draws and hitting mosquitos on the fly, the true secret of the gunfighter was in going with your instincts first when they told you the other fool really meant it.

So Longarm was ready for it when the older and now ashen-faced man they all knew as Sheriff Wallward went for his gun. The contest wasn't even close as Longarm drew and fired once in hopes of taking at least one of the bastards alive.

He hoped in vain. His two hundred grains of lead took his target smack in the breadbasket to slam him back and bounce him forward off the bar to land flat on his face in the sawdust at Longarm's feet.

Longarm rolled him faceup with one boot. The cuss was staring wide-eyed but blowing bloody bubbles out his nose. When Longarm saw the dying man wasn't bothered by the sawdust sticking to one open eye, he knew it would be a waste of time to ask him how he felt.

Longarm whirled as he heard Ed Skane snap, "The man said to stay out of it, Clem!" and saw the storekeeper was covering another of the dead sheriff's deputies.

Longarm announced, "This wasn't Sheriff Walter Wallward. So he was elected under false pretenses and that don't count."

He saw the two Skane boys were there with their old lawman dad. So he snapped, "Robert Skane and Alexander Skane, you are hereby deputies pro tem as federal lawmen. I want the two of you to run over to what you know as the Wallward house and arrest the lady you've always known as Flo Wallward. Be gentle with her and just hold her there. She's a crippled old gal who's led a hard life, and I'm hoping she'll tie up some loose ends for us after I've pointed out I don't have to charge her with murder in the first if she'd like to turn state's evidence. She may have been out to poison me earlier, but what the hell."

The two youths hesitated till their father, still holding a gun on a deputy who was likely innocent, growled, "You heard the man, boys. Get cracking!"

They left, doubtless chagrined to miss the rest of it as Longarm turned to the coroner, casualy reloading that one spent round, and suggested, "Mayhaps I'd best start at the very beginning?"

The coroner said he sure wished someone would. So Longarm held his six-gun down his right leg as he began. "Once upon a time there was a fair federal deputy with a drinking problem and a green hand Marshall Billy Vail had asked him to break in. Need I add the drinker was the real Walter Wallward or that I was his green backup?"

"Then who's that bleeding on the floor?" demanded a voice in the crowd, followed by a puzzled murmur.

Longarm said, "I'll never get to that if you gents don't shut up and listen tight. If I may have the floor, it was seven years ago that U.S. Deputy Wallward shot it out with the three Plowright brothers in Julesberg, Colorado, backed up by me and Deputies Pope and Gilchrist, who are no longer with us. Gilchrist got arrowed by Arapaho along the South Platte, and Pope lost an argument with train robbers down by Trinidad. But first we buried the Plowright brothers. All three of 'em."

The local deputy called Clem protested, "Then who's that tall drink of water who just hung his fool self in our lockup?"

Longarm said, "I ain't going to finish this already complicated tale if you gents keep horning in. I was confounded by all those odd conflicting notions, till I finally shaved off the last big lie that had been staring me in the face from the beginning. So shut up and take my word I can back up most of what I'll be saying as I try to keep things simple enough to grasp."

Ed Skane said he wished Longarm would. So Longarm continued. "Like I said, poor Walt Wallward had this drinking problem. He was what they call a periodical drunk. He was a fine lawman when he was sober but once he'd had a few too many, watch out! So Billy Vail decided, and I had to agree, nobody like that ought to be inflicted upon the general public with a loaded gun and a federal badge. He let old Walt go and that's the last I know for sure about him. I'm hoping old Flo will be willing to fill in a few missing details."

He caught himself reaching absently for a cheroot, decided this was neither the time nor place, and went on. "I've solid evidence that once he'd been handed the shovel old Walt sobered up enough, from time to time, to compose a long and somewhat tedious autobiography. He likely hoped to have it published, like the more exciting autobiography of Buffalo Bill written by Ned Buntline."

Someone murmured, "I read that one. It was a pisser."

Longarm silenced the crowd with a frown. "The one old Walt wrote was slow reading but mighty detailed and, far as I know, accurate. So somebody taking the time to read all the way through it more than once could hope to pass for the real Walt Wallward, the famous lawman, provided he looked at all like the cuss and didn't meet up with too many folks who knew the real thing well or recently."

An older gent Longarm had last seen on the coroner's panel at that other hearing chimed in. "Hot damn! Silas Mullens said he'd met an old-timer passing through with some stock who'd allowed the Walt Wallward he'd known a spell back had been another face entirely!"

Longarm shook his head and said, "Silas would have printed it if they'd been *certain*. He'd only cast *doubts* on an incumbent sheriff's ability and brag before he was murdered, and you're making me get ahead of myself again, damn it!"

They fell silent and he continued. "While the real Walt Wallward was drifting about, getting drunk, working at odd jobs, and writing his tedious autobiography, there was this train wreck down in Texas. A no-longer-young but still pretty stage actress and other members of her theatrical troupe got banged up pretty good. One was a right tall stage magician of a striking appearance but smooth shaven and not scarred up, till after that train wreck. It took many a wire to many a theatrical booking agent, including some old Flo had forgotten to write down for me. Then, once I found out she'd once worked with a stage magician years before, I still failed to fit anything together for the simple reason that nobody I could get in my sights as a suspect seemed to have any damned motive!"

Ed Skane asked, "Wasn't it murder?"

Longarm replied, "Not directly. Getting back to Texas, a whole bunch of no-longer-young and never-all-that-successful folks met up in some flea-bitten hotel or boardinghouse. Old Walt got this crippled actress to read his manuscript. She may have had nothing better to read, or she may have already noticed how closely the real lawman resembled her husband, lover, pimp, or maybe she'll tell us."

The old horse doctor had investigated a crime or more, although never anything this serious, so he was the one who declared, "I can see how they might have made the switch, but *why*, for the love of the Great Horned Spoon?"

Longarm said, "I reckon it was for the love of money. It's tough to remember how desperate you can feel when you're broke the minute you have a few dimes to rub together. But we're talking down and out in Texas, with no job skills that would qualify older white folks for a decent job. They might have been planning on heading up this way in any case. The Montana Gold Rush was on, and stock raising was way safer after the Fifth Cav finished avenging the Seventh at the expense of Mister Lo, the Poor Indian."

Ed Skane said, "That's about when me and mine come up here from the Indian Nation. I remember Walt Wallward, or that mess on the floor, being the big frog in this little puddle as we arrived."

Longarm said, "Flo ought to be able to tell us whatever happened to the real Walt Wallward. I hope he just drank himself to death. I don't see how we'll be able to let her off if it was something he ate. In any event, they wound up here in this one-horse town, no offense, and as soon as the rest of you incorporated the surrounding range as a territorial county he ran for sheriff, and being such a famous lawman, or being Skane here was so modest, guess who got elected?"

Skane grumbled, "I voted for him, the more fool I! He had *me* convinced he'd ridden for the Justice Department, and damn it, so had I!"

Longarm said soothingly, "He was likely a stage actor to begin with, and the thing about actors is that you never know when they're pretending to be somebody else. Thanks to the real Wallward's copious writings, and Lord knows how many other books he'd had time to read, he found it easy enough to play a convincing sheriff with the help of real cowboy deputies and a vigilance committee capable of scaring off any serious trouble."

The coroner objected. "Hold on. Our sheriff, whoever he was, kept ordering Lester Kenmore to disband his night riders."

From the back of the crowd Lester Kenmore protested, "I heard that, and I'll have you know we rode as often in broad-ass daylight with no masks."

Longarm said, "Shut up, Les. I was fixing to point out this famous dead lawman never *did* anything when you and your boys went right on acting silly. That was a clue, had only I been looking closer at what I thought was an old pal. But forget how good a sheriff this imposter made, and let's get to Silas Mullens and the Grangers hankering to run some other candidate this fall."

The coroner shot the cadaver on the floor a dirty look and flatly stated, "They murdered Silas Mullens and all those other poor souls to keep him from printing the truth in his populist paper!"

Longarm shook his head and said, "They were after me. Mullens didn't know the truth. That was where I came in, and that was why they were out to get rid of me once I'd done the chore they wanted of me but before I might guess the truth myself."

Pointing at the mighty blank face at his feet, Longarm told them, "Silas Mullens and doubtless others were starting to sniff at their sheriff's past in hopes of digging dirt on the real Walt Wallward. He'd already taken the pledge at the behest of his fine little wife, in case anyone recalled his other self as a hopeless drunk down Denver way. But they were naturally sweating bullets about an actual challenge to his true identity. So they took an educated risk aimed at making any notion he was an imposter seem ridiculous. They brought in a more obvious imposter, along with other sneaks of stage or saddle-bum background. They had their tall old pal from their salad days show up as a menacing but piss-poor imitation of a long-dead outlaw. Then, after the fake Tall Tom had half persuaded Silas Mullens the sheriff had to be the real Walt Wallward to rate such an outlandish enemy, they sent for me, an old junior deputy of the real Walt Wallward, to come up here and help an old pal expose another imposter entirely!"

Ed Skane said firmly, "That took brass balls, or lunacy. No fake could look enough like another man to fool a real pal!"

But Longarm said, "He did. Close enough, leastways, when you consider I'd ridden with a puffy-faced drunk a few times without becoming engaged to him long ago and far away. Looking back to my first meeting with this fake, I do remember thinking sobering up and settling down had made him look a whole lot prettier than I'd been picturing. But in case I'd failed to buy the masquerade they'd already menaced me over in Helena, in front of the local law, just in case they had to account for my sudden death before it might be a better time to kill me."

The deputy called Clem nodded and exclaimed, "He told all of us you'd brushed with toughs called Dakota and Santee and ordered us to watch out for strangers answering to their descriptions."

Longarm said, "He doubtless described them a mite awry, judging by the way they got to ride all over creation. At any rate, distracted by that apparently pointless brush with sinister strangers, and then meeting up with another stranger who kept trying to tell me he was a dead man, I simply accepted an older, slimmer, more distinguished bullshit artist as a man I'd ridden under years before. He had his answers down pat, and I naturally never expected to recognize a wife I knew I was meeting for the first time. Looking back, it was dumb of me to buy her memories of an old fellow deputy pulling himself back together down in Texas. It was a mistake, in the end, for her to send me to bed with a copy of that tedious autobiography. I reckon it was to show how much my old pal, Walt, admired me. I was flattered some in that part about the shootout with the Plowright boys, and you know what they say about catching flies with honey."

Ed Skane was no longer covering Clem. Longarm decided it was safe to holster his own gun as he continued. "Let's just allow I took the bait like a born sucker and set out to prove the fake Tall Tom was the only fake in these parts. I'd accidently made friends with the Mullens family by saving Miss Bathsheba Mullens from them half-baked kidnappers. This dead skunk and his bunch had nothing to do with that. But a born opportunist does what he can with what fortune offers. He was expecting me to ask the wrong questions from his point of view at any moment. So when he saw I had even his political enemies convinced he was the real Walt Wallward, with a real rep as a fair lawman, it was time for me to get killed by those mysterious owlhoots, Dakota and Santee. We know what a shitty job they did. So set them to one side and join me as I tell my gracious hosts I've been invited to supper at the Mullens house. They set up young MacTaggert or some other underling to spoil our supper with dynamite. Then, knowing yet another confederate who knew what was really going on would surely be a prime suspect, they arranged to have the fake Tall Tom Plowright appear to be getting arrested about the time they blew us up at the far end of the valley. This fake Walt Wallward must have shit his pants when I showed up at the so-called Plowright claim just as their infernal device went off. But say what you will about his sheriffing, he was one hell of an actor. I never suspected toad squat as we went through the charade of taking the sinister Tall Tom in on suspicion."

Clem said, "*I* sure thought he was real. But hold on. If that tall prisoner was really in cahoots with our sheriff all the time, how did he wind up so dead in his cell?"

Longarm said, "They had to kill him to shut him up. Or so they thought when they failed a second time to blow me up at yet another supper table. They were sort of monotonous as criminals, but remember they started out as stage actors, accustomed to repeating good lines. I'd done what I'd been sent for to do. But I still didn't know that made me the only target anyone was really interested in. Like a fool I kept worrying about a nice old couple being menaced in ways that made no sense no matter how many odds and ends I uncovered. I kept trying to slice away unimportant distractions with an imaginary razor, but as long as I kept thinking I was helping the real Walt Wallward, I just didn't know what to slice away."

Clem suggested, "Tell us about that gunfight with the one called Dakota over to Helena."

Longarm shook his head and said, "I told you they weren't all that important, next to their mastermind here on the floor. I never shot it out with Dakota. I suckered him in the dark and had the drop on him. It was likely the one called Santee who gunned him to shut him up, even as he was lying through his teeth to me. But I modestly reckon that somewhere in the back of my devious mind I was starting to wonder how secret enemies seemed to know so much about my movements when I hadn't discussed 'em with the whole world.

Not sure who might be blabbing to whom, I commenced to play my cards closer to my vest. I forgot to tell the sheriff I was bluffing when I tried to throw a scare into his mysterious prisoner with a serious charge up Canada way. It got him to make one slip about where he really might have come from. That other fake on the floor knew enough about such matters by then to know I'd surely check with the law back in Elkton, Maryland, if ever I got near a telegraph wire again alive."

He frowned thoughtfully down at the body as he mused aloud, "I just can't say why I didn't feel right about going home to supper with a pal. I know what I had in mind when I let others hear me say I'd be supping with Ed Skane there. You might consider old Ed as a write-in candidate for sheriff now. He's got two good deputies who call him Dad already."

Skane muttered, "Aw, mush!" as everyone else seemed to find that a grand suggestion.

Longarm said, "When that dynamite went off in the street instead of where he'd told MacTaggert to heave it, this rascal knew I was still alive and doubtless starting to get serious about all this shit. So he and the one called Santee joined the bigger but unsuspecting fake Tall Tom in his cell and strangled him. The strongest man goes weak and blacks out suddenly with a braided belt crushing the arteries to his brain and somebody else holding both his hands tight. Then they strung him up to make it look like a suicide and split up amid all the confusion. I'll never be certain whether the one called Santee had orders to gun me or simply grabbed for the brass ring when I seemed to recognize him. You all heard the shots down this way, and you all saw how your sheriff acted when I came in, alive as ever, to tell him I was ready to make an arrest. I was partly bluffing. I wasn't sure he was the last of the bunch until he showed me he was by assuming I had to mean him. Up until I knew he was fixing to draw, I was only sure he was a ringer. It only occurred to me he had to be a ringer as I was observing most anyone can look like a Santee to a fool who's not certain what a Santee looks like. The minute I applied that imaginary razor to the blowsy old drunk I'd only known a short time long ago, all the pieces seemed to fall in place like magic. I had more than all the facts I needed. They just never fit together till I saw how a lawman with no motive to kill another lawman he'd put on the case himself had every reason in the world to kill me before I cracked it!"

Chapter 13

It was raining in Denver a few days later as Longarm came into the front office dripping water off his dark slicker and sopping Stetson. So Henry looked up from behind his typewriter to blandly ask, "Is it raining outside?"

Longarm soberly replied, "Why, no, Henry. I got pissed on out in the hall by one of them stenographer gals. She was hanging from a ceiling fixture with nothing under her petticoat, the sassy thing."

Henry sighed wearily and said, "You'd better hang that wet slicker out here. Marshal Vail gets sore enough when you drip ashes on his carpet. He's been expecting you for some time. So watch it."

Longarm hung up his dripping hat while he was at it, and lit a cheroot outside before he ambled inside in no worse than a damp tweed suit and squishy boots.

The squat Marshal Vail behind the desk shot a disgusted look at the banjo clock on his oak-paneled wall, swung his bullet head to stare out the window, and said, "I hate fall weather out this way. Getting up in the morning a man never knows whether he'll be sun-fried, rain-soaked, or snow-blinded by the end of the day."

Longarm sat down, uninvited as ever, and mildly observed, "I hope it lets up. There's a Sunday-Go-to-Meeting-on-the-Green planned for this weekend with a cake raffle and some square dancing afterwards.

Vail growled, "I'm sure you'll wind up with a gal who bakes good too. If I can interest you at all in your damned job, we just got in some confirmation on a heap of guesswork on your part. You realize, I hope, what a pickle you'd have been in had you slapped leather on the real Walt Wallward?"

Longarm took a thoughtful drag on his smoke and decided, "Oh, I might have beaten him to the draw, as long as he'd been killing his nervous system with booze. I never drew on that fake sheriff up in Wolverine before he made his own move. I hate to give anyone such an edge. But I had to be sure, and I was pretty sure he was a stage actor who'd done all his killing mighty sneaky."

"My all-points queries by longer night letters tell me his real name was Hamilton Mooreheart, a trick rope artist on the wicked stage."

Longarm snorted, "His stage name, you mean. Nobody would really be sprinkled Hamilton Mooreheart."

Vail shrugged. "I'll not pester you with the real name of the Amazing Abdulla, assisted in his feats of magic by the adorable Florence Feathersham. You guessed right about that man commencing his wild career as a Tidewater farm boy. That Flo gal too, when she was first starting out back East before the war. I'll bet they never figured anyone would connect her in her old age to a tall magician she'd been traveling with a good thirty years back. The railroad underwriters say the magical monster put in a handsome claim for the loss of his ability to palm live birds with his big left paw after he was in a train wreck that ended the graceful entrances and exits of a somewhat younger Florence Feathersham. The trick roper she was never married up with formally wasn't hurt as bad in that wreck, but as you'd guessed, none of them were getting any younger, none of them were ever fixing to make it to Broadway or even Market Street out Frisco way, and how old and gray can a stage cowboy get before his audience starts laughing in the wrong places?"

"I had all that in my report," Longarm sighed with an anxious look out the window. It was still raining fire and salt, but the sky seemed a little brighter and with any luck things might clear up by quitting time.

Vail said, "All right, you done good and guessed right for a change, you lucky cuss. If you were planning on whipping up to that certain brownstone mansion up on Capitol Hill before this office is supposed to close for the day, be advised my old woman has her spies keeping an eye on that young widow woman who ought to be ashamed of herself."

Longarm replied sincerely that he hadn't been planning on pestering that particular old pal. It was nobody's business how he'd wound up stuck with another pal entirely who tended to get shrill when she felt neglected—although he doubted old Edwina Rose would really go after another lady with those pinking shears as she'd suggested she might.

Vail told him Henry had some court orders for him to serve, rain or shine. So Longarm rose to leave. Vail warned him not to go anywhere else in downtown Denver with those court orders.

Longarm laughed and said there was no place to get laid in downtown Denver without paying for it. Vail didn't seem to find it at all amusing when Longarm added nobody could afford a boot shine, let alone a blow job, on what such a cheap outfit paid a poor cuss.

Out in the front office, Henry said the papers weren't back from Judge Dickerson yet. Longarm said he didn't care. His relaxed ways seemed to irritate the prissy clerk, who smiled sort of dirty and said, "By the way, I heard some disturbing gossip while you were up Montana way, Don Juan. You know that Miss Edwina Rose you'd been carrying on with for some time?"

Longarm blew a casual smoke ring and didn't answer. He knew Henry was busting with something, and sure enough, Henry said, "She went to the Harvest Moon Cotillion with another swain entirely! He drives a Fisher surrey with his own horse and owns his own drugstore. His name is Ralph Applegate if you want to bust him up."

Longarm smiled innocently and asked, "Now why would I want to do a thing like that, Henry?"

The clerk looked puzzled and replied, "Weren't you paying attention to me just now? A sissy druggist has stolen your girl! There's more to the story than that one fancy dance. They've been seen all over town ever since. He's had her to Romero's for Eye-talian noodles, and they were seen swapping spit in the back row of the Apollo Hall while *The Maid of Croissey* was still in its first act, and—don't go fussing at the messenger—some say she'd been sort of helping him close up his drugstore after dark, and they say he has quarters right upstairs."

Longarm had just said the druggist was welcome to such a fickle little thing when Miss Bubbles, from the stenographers' pool down the hall, came in with those court orders and a mighty flirtatious smile. Miss Bubbles wasn't the bitty blonde's real name. It derived from the way she was built. But when she demurely suggested Longarm walk her back to her office if he was going that way, he politely said he had to get these important papers delivered the other way.

When the spectacular Miss Bubbles left with a disappointed sigh, Henry chuckled and said, "You must be planning to pistol-whip that druggist. Weren't you the one who told me one time there was nothing like a pretty gal to help a man get over a pretty gal?"

Longarm smiled thoughtfully and replied, "There's pretty and then there's lovely, Henry. I figured after work I'd just mosey up Capitol Hill to admire the beautiful view."

Henry said, "You won't see much if this rain keeps up."

Henry was always saying things like that. He'd never viewed a certain young widow woman with her long brown hair let down in candlelight, once he let her get on top.

Watch for

LONGARM AND THE BOUNTY OF BLOOD

181st in the bold LONGARM series
from Jove

Coming in January!

LONGARM

Explore the exciting Old West with
one of the men who made it wild!